FIRED

Her heart thumped hard against her ribcage and her whole body tingled with awareness at his close proximity.

The next second his hands had found her face and slid along her jaw, drawing her towards him, and then his mouth was on hers, hot and firm.

He dropped kisses along her jawline, sending great twists of erotic sensation through her whole body.

'Don't think,' he murmured, the vibration of his words tickling and teasing the hypersensitive skin of her throat as he moved lower. 'Just *do*.'

He slammed against her, forcing her back against the wall, sending what sounded like brooms crashing to the floor.

This wasn't playful any more. It was hot and heavy and serious.

Inevitable.

It was what she wanted. What she *needed*.

In a shocking moment of clarity she realised that this had always been going to happen.

She

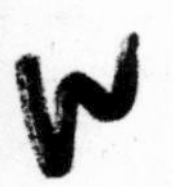

Published in Great Britain 2014
by Mills & Boon, an imprint of Harlequin (UK) Limited,
Eton House, 18-24 Paradise Road, Richmond, Surrey, TW9 1SR

ISBN: 978-0-263-91158-9

Harlequin (UK) Limited's policy is to use papers that are natural, renewable and recyclable products and made from wood grown in sustainable forests. The logging and manufacturing processes conform to the legal environmental regulations of the country of origin.

Printed and bound in Spain
by Blackprint CPI, Barcelona

BK (Before Kids) **Christy McKellen** worked as a video and radio producer in London and Nottingham. After a decade of dealing with nappies, tantrums and endless questions from toddlers she has come out the other side and moved into the wonderful world of literature. She now spends her time writing flirty, sexy romance with a kick—her dream job!

Christy loves to hear from readers. You can contact her at christy@christymckellen.com, through her website: www.christymckellen.com, via Facebook: www.facebook.com/christymckellenauthor or on Twitter: www.twitter.com/ChristyMcKellen

Other Modern Tempted™ titles by Christy McKellen:

LESSONS IN RULE-BREAKING
HOLIDAY WITH A STRANGER

This and other titles by Christy McKellen are also available as eBooks from www.millsandboon.co.uk

DEDICATION

Big thanks go to my friend Rhiannon,
for that lightbulb moment in the pub.

Also to my friend Sophie, for undergoing the tough job of researching London cocktail bars with me.

And of course to Tom, for helping me plot and plan in the Spanish sunshine over coffee and cake.

CHAPTER ONE

TALLULAH LAZENBY DRAINED the last drop of her large glass of Sauvignon Blanc and clung onto the comforting buzz of the alcohol, until the feeling dissipated and her nerves returned.

She really shouldn't be drinking the night before her grievance meeting with the owner of the radio station where she worked as a DJ—a job that had, until recently, made her rise with excitement every morning—but she needed something to dull the growing panic that tomorrow could be her last day of work there.

'Lula, snap out of it. It's going to be okay,' her friend Emily muttered into her ear, clicking her fingers in front of her face and dragging her out of her agitated funk and into the here and now of the dimly lit Covent Garden pub, where they were celebrating a friend's birthday.

Lula gave her a tight-lipped smile. 'Easy for you to say; you didn't make the catastrophic mistake of sleeping with your Station Manager and scuppering your chances at career advancement when you refused to be his regular sex-puppet.'

Emily tried to keep a straight face, but failed spectacularly. 'I have to say, Lu, it wasn't one of your best moves.'

She shot her friend a *no kidding* grimace.

'Lord knows what possessed you to sleep with *him*,' Emily added.

Lula nodded solemnly into her empty glass.

Jeremy—or Jez as he preferred to be called—was an overconfident, self-absorbed philanderer and the exact opposite of what she was looking for in a long-term partner.

'It was after a *very* long, *very* dry patch and he caught me at a moment of weakness,' she muttered, her face hot with the ignominy of how it had cast a dark shadow over their working relationship when she'd told him in no uncertain terms that there wasn't going to be a repeat performance.

Jez was not the type of man you said *no* to.

And she'd paid the price for it.

After a few weeks of stilted and antagonistic interaction, he'd blithely informed her that he would no longer be moving her onto the Breakfast Show—even though he'd been promising to for months. And, just to rub salt in the wound, he was giving her Drivetime Show to Darla—one of the other female DJs at the station—who apparently had no qualms about regularly bumping uglies with him.

So now she was just supposed to float around the station, covering for other presenters when they needed time off from their shows.

A major step backwards on her career path.

'At least the owner's taking your complaint seriously,' Emily said, sprawling back in her chair and licking a bit of lemon off the rim of her glass of vodka and tonic.

Lula put her head in her hands and stared down at the table. 'I didn't tell you the worst bit. I found out today that Jez's *daddy* is best buddies with the owner.

There's no way he'll take my side on this. Not when the Old Boy Network is in play.' She rubbed her eyes and groaned, 'Nepotism sucks.'

The corner of her friend's mouth twitched up into a consoling smile. 'It'll be okay. You're the best DJ that station has; they're not about to let you walk—have some faith in yourself.'

'Hmph.'

Emily leaned forward and slapped an encouraging hand onto Lula's leg. 'You know what you need to do right now? Give yourself a confidence boost so you can stride in there tomorrow with your head held high.'

Lula flashed her friend a pained look. 'How am I meant to do that, exactly?'

'You could start by engaging in some power-flirting with a crazy-hot sex god.' Emily gave one of the trademark saucy winks that had earned her legions of fans on her popular *Treasure Trail* TV show.

Lula spluttered in mirth. 'Do they even exist? 'Coz I've never met one.'

Emily crossed her arms and shook her head sadly. 'You know, if you took some time out from your tireless quest to find this mythical "perfect man" and just indulged in a bit of fun—with someone other than your boss, that is—perhaps you'd get your mojo back?' She cocked a chastising eyebrow, before turning away to answer a question one of the other birthday guests called across to her.

Lula snorted at the back of her friend's head, but accepted that Emily had a point. She probably *should* give herself a break and stop worrying about finding *The One*, but it had been one disappointing relationship after another recently and she was beginning to panic that she was destined to be single for ever.

Hence the foolish move of sleeping with her boss.

She'd just celebrated her thirty-first birthday—which *both* of her parents had managed to forget about this year—and Jez had been so attentive, so seemingly sympathetic, that she'd found herself succumbing to his determined advances.

And look what had happened.

She was *never* making that mistake again. Sleeping with colleagues was a fool's game. It only ever ended in tears and awkwardness. And possibly unemployment.

If only she didn't find it so nerve-racking talking to men she found attractive. It was much easier to connect with people when she was behind her microphone. If a conversation was going badly on-air and she was floundering, she could cut them off by playing a song or going to an ad break—snatching some time to pull herself together—and nobody was any the wiser. She'd also got into the habit of pre-recording interviews so she could edit them later and pushing her listeners to send a text or tweet to the show, instead of calling in.

Recently it had seemed as though her show on *Flash FM* was the only place she had a modicum of control. Out in the real world her deep-seated shyness, stemming from way back in her youth, often made her blurt out stupid things or induced one of her humiliating brain freezes and her mortification would show clearly on her face for all to see.

'Rabbit caught in headlights' was not a good look on her.

She glanced around the bar, her gaze snagging on a cosy-looking couple to her right. She experienced a sting of jealousy as they giggled at some private joke together.

Was it really too much to ask to meet someone who

was genuinely interested in making *her* the centre of their universe, getting married some day and starting a family? Something she'd been dreaming about since her own dysfunctional family had come apart at the seams.

Her chest gave an uncomfortable lurch. No. This was not the time to start dwelling on her less than perfect childhood.

'Hey, Lu, speaking of sex gods, check out the guy sitting behind us,' Emily murmured into Lula's ear, her hot, boozy breath tickling the hairs on her neck.

Intrigued, Lula swivelled round to get an eyeful of the guy Emily was talking about. She could only make out his broad back and a hint of his profile because he was turned away from her, but she could see exactly what had caught her friend's interest.

The textbook triangular shape of his torso stretched his expensive-looking shirt to perfection, giving a tantalising suggestion of the ripped body concealed underneath.

Lula would bet her life he could be found sweating away in the gym every morning before setting off for some high-powered job. Something about his self-possessed posture made her think he was somebody *big* somewhere. You just got a feeling from people like him.

Power and control.

The skin on the back of his neck between the crisp collar of his shirt and the clean, razored cut of his dark, short back and sides haircut was tanned a warm honey colour, as if he'd just got back from a holiday in the sun. Lula could picture him, stretched out on the golden sand in just a tiny pair of swimmers, his body shimmering with perspiration in the intense midday sun.

Ooh.

The buzz from the glass of wine returned, only this

time it washed a deep satisfying heat through a much more intimate part of her body.

Good grief, if just a flash of his skin could do that to her, imagine what would happen if she got to speak to him face to face.

Spontaneous combustion, probably.

A crazy idea struck her that made her heart thump heavily against her chest. Perhaps she should practice the façade of kick-ass poise and self-assurance that she was going to need at tomorrow's meeting on him. She could buy him a drink, then plonk herself down at his table as if she chatted up dishy men every day. She just needed to draw on the confidence she summoned to perform on the radio and she could become the out-going woman everyone expected her to be in real life.

At work she got past any awkwardness at meeting new people by researching her subjects thoroughly and planning her questions, but she didn't have the time or tools for that right now. This would have to be a study in improvisation.

She would fake it till she made it with this guy.

Even the suggestion of 'making it' with him sent an-other zingy little frisson deep into her pelvis.

Just flirting, Lula—that's all that's gonna happen here.

Okay. Time to get her game face on.

If she could succeed at capturing the interest of a handsome man in a bar tonight, she could damn well persuade the station owner to give her a fair hearing tomorrow.

Tonight, audience, I'm going to be Tallulah Lazenby—top rated DJ at Flash FM, *social mover and shaker and loquacious livewire.*

She sat up straighter in her seat.

Yes. Positivity. That's the ticket.

Powered by that rousing resolve, she grabbed her bag and got up, centring herself on her six-inch heels, and primed herself to shimmy on past the sex god and over to the bar.

Tristan Bamfield winced and placed his empty beer bottle onto the sticky pub table with a firm *clunk* as the group of women sitting behind him let out another squall of high-pitched laughter.

Usually he wouldn't stray from the hotel bar when he was working away from home, but he'd found himself needing to escape from the over-zealous attentions of a primped-to-within-an-inch-of-her-life Sloaney who'd zeroed in on him, and this dimly lit traditional London pub, with its purple and black painted walls and trendily scuffed up leather sofas and painted tables, had seemed like the perfect refuge.

Until this vociferous band of banshees had followed him in shortly afterwards, that was.

All he'd wanted was one quiet drink before going back to the cold solitude of his hotel room but it seemed that peace was the last thing he was likely to get in here.

Bah humbug.

He knew he was being uncharitable—he wasn't usually averse to a bit of lively banter—but he'd been plagued by a vague sense of irritation ever since his father had convinced him—by way of passive aggressive joshing—to come to London and sort out some seedy-sounding mess at his vanity project of a radio station while he swanned around the Middle East on a honeymoon with his fifth wife.

What a total farce.

Tristan hadn't even bothered going to the wedding,

knowing full well this marriage wasn't likely to last long either. He'd made sure to buy them the most expensive present on their wedding list, though—his way of acknowledging the union and mitigating any potential hard feelings about his no-show. He didn't dislike his new stepmother—he'd barely even met her—but he couldn't bring himself to summon up the fake smiles and phoney enthusiasm required at these events any more.

He twisted the empty bottle between his hands and turned his thoughts to the situation at the radio station instead, not wanting to waste any more time dwelling on his father's irrepressible addiction to nuptials.

It seemed that one of the DJs, Tallulah something-or-other, claimed the Station Manager had reneged on a promise to promote her to Breakfast Show presenter and had also taken her off her current show when she refused to sleep with him. The manager, on the other hand, swore blind she was lying and angry with him after he'd disciplined her for turning up to work drunk.

The whole thing had a sickeningly sordid air about it.

Added into the mix was the fact that Jeremy, the Station Manager, was the son of a good friend of the family and his father wanted the DJ fired to keep relations cordial between them.

Tristan knew from past experience of working with his old man at the family business that he was often too quick to take the more *convenient* way out of a problem instead of taking time to look at the whole picture.

He needed to be careful here.

Sighing, he rubbed a hand over his face, trying to relieve his building frustration.

He really didn't need this right now.

After taking the last couple of months to get his head

together following a humiliating end to a four-year relationship, he just wanted to be left alone to settle back into what was left of his life in Edinburgh.

Fat chance of that.

One of the women from the table behind him sidled past, distracting him from his thoughts as her fresh floral scent hit his nose. He watched as she click-clicked away on ludicrously high heels, her shapely rear swaying provocatively from side to side as she headed towards the bar.

Despite his resolution to steer clear of women until he'd got his head straight again, he couldn't help but be captivated by her petite, curvy figure. It made him think of an Amazonian woman in miniature—all delicious voluptuousness and sexual potency.

He watched idly as she waited for the barman to notice her, appearing to sink against the high, solid wood counter the longer she was ignored, until her previously upright posture had dipped down into a full-on slouch.

There was a particular kind of dejection to her body language that made him sit up and take notice.

It reminded him of the time right after Marcy told him she was throwing away what he now thought of as their joke of a relationship, and he'd felt as though someone had stripped the blood, guts and air out of him.

He'd bought her everything she'd ever wanted—designer clothes, a sports car, ludicrously expensive jewellery—but it still hadn't been enough for her.

She'd taken it all with her when she'd left him, of course.

The heat of his humiliation washed through him for the thousandth time since she'd dropped the bombshell, leaving a jittery sense of unease. He'd known for a while that things hadn't exactly been perfect between them, but he couldn't forgive all the lying and sneaking around behind his back that she'd done.

The two of them must have thought he was a real chump.

As if the dark power of his thoughts had somehow penetrated through to her own, the woman at the bar seemed to pull herself together and she straightened her posture, giving a little jump in her heels as if to remind herself to stand tall—which, judging by her diminutive height, he guessed was something she'd probably done ever since she'd stopped growing.

He really should get back to the hotel, and get stuck into the mound of paperwork that waited for him there, but something kept his gaze fixed to the woman's skinny-jeans-clad rear view.

She had very long light brown hair pulled back into a loose ponytail at the nape of her neck, which swung like a pendulum as she jiggled on the spot. He bet she had a cute little nose and huge, sensual eyes too, which would draw him into a world of *what the hell* the moment he looked into them.

Had he guessed right?

The thought of leaving now without at least catching a glimpse of what she actually looked like was curiously unthinkable. Suddenly, he really needed to know for sure, to reassure himself that he wasn't *totally* ignorant when it came to reading women, as Marcy had so unsubtly suggested.

Getting up from his chair, he strode over to where she stood at the bar. Maybe he'd have one more drink before he went back to the hotel. After all, he was in for a pretty dull night on his own, so he might as well get his kicks where he could.

Rubbing a hand over his forehead, he sighed to himself. He *must* be feeling jaded if he was resorting to playing *guess my face* in a place like this.

Apparently she heard his sigh because she glanced round to look at him, surprise flaring in her deep-set cornflower-blue eyes.

It was as if he'd caught her out. Perhaps she'd been eyeing him up earlier too?

The thought warmed him.

As she opened her mouth to draw breath, something must have caught in her throat because she paused for a moment, her eyes widening in panic, before letting out a forcible choking cough. Tearing her distressed gaze from his, she clamped her hand around her mouth in mortification.

She was prettier than he'd imagined—in an endearing girl-next-door way that made him want to lean over and rub her back to stop the coughing fit. To take care of her.

That was what he did best, after all—took care of people. Until they turned around and stabbed him in the back, that was.

He shook the negative thought off and grinned at her, attempting to project concern with his expression.

She gave him a watery-eyed smile back and flapped a hand in his direction as if asking for his forgiveness.

'You okay?' he asked.

She nodded, her gaze not quite meeting his. 'Fine,' she rasped out finally. 'Something went the wrong way.' She gestured towards her throat and his gaze followed where her finger indicated.

She had beautifully creamy skin, with a smattering of small dark moles just west of the hollow of her throat. A strange impulse to stroke his fingers across them gripped him. He'd probably make her choke in shock again if he did. He almost tried it, just to see if his theory was borne out.

When his gaze returned to her face he noticed two spots of colour had appeared on her high-set cheekbones.

Cute.

He could see now why she favoured such high heels too; even with them on, the top of her head only just reached past his shoulders.

She was studying him warily, as if trying to decide whether to spend more of her precious time talking to him. Clearly she deemed him worthy because she said, 'I'm Lu,' and put out a small, delicately boned hand for him to shake.

He took it, his own looking obscenely monstrous in comparison. He was afraid for a second he might crush her if he wasn't careful.

'Short for Louise?' he asked.

She smiled back and opened her mouth to speak but, before she could, a harried-looking barman came over and leaned in towards her, suddenly eager to take her order.

She asked for a glass of wine before turning to him and murmuring, 'Buy you a drink…?' She raised her eyebrows in a double question, asking for his name as well as his answer.

Whoa, that *voice*. It made him think all kinds of inappropriate thoughts as it lapped indecently through his head.

'Tristan. Tristan Bamfield.' He shook her a curt *no thanks* in response to her offer of a drink, reluctant to get into anything more than a passing conversation. The thought of being dragged over and introduced to the gaggle of women she'd been sitting with made him feel faintly woozy.

She nodded in an odd, knowing kind of way, but apparently had other ideas about what he *actually* wanted, adding a bottle of the beer he'd been drinking to her order.

He caught her eye when she glanced back at him. 'You noticed what I was drinking?'

'I'm good with details,' she said, flashing him a coy smile.

'That's a useful skill.'

She shrugged. 'It's moderately useful. Not like having superior strength or the ability to see into the future or anything. Now *that* would be useful.'

Yeah. If *he'd* been able to see into the future he could have circumnavigated the total train wreck of his last relationship.

The barman returned with their drinks and he watched Lu hand over the cash in silence, feeling a niggling discomfort about her buying him a drink. She gestured towards his beer. 'For coughing all over you.'

Tristan smiled. 'Unnecessary, but thanks.' Picking up the bottle, he took a long swig.

Lu did the same with her wine, the large glass looking enormous in her dinky hand.

'I see they do wine by the pint here,' he said, nodding towards the glass. 'That drink's almost as big as you are.'

He caught a flash of what looked like startled irritation before she converted it to wry amusement. 'Yeah, well, you get quality with me, not quantity,' she said, a steely edge creeping into her voice. 'And I thought real men drank beer from pint glasses, not namby-pamby little bottles.' She flashed him a disparaging grin.

He raised an amused eyebrow back. He'd annoyed her, he could tell, but she wasn't making an excuse and moving away—she was taking him on.

The woman had grit by the truckload.

He liked that about her. He liked it a lot.

In fact, now he thought about it, she was the first woman to pique his interest since Marcy had left him.

Taking a step towards him, Lu looked up directly into his face, her gaze roaming over his hair, his eyes, snagging on his mouth.

There was something in her expression that made his libido sit up and take notice. He smiled, feeling the intensity of their attraction heat his blood.

Something akin to determination was playing across her face, as if she was having some sort of internal fight with herself.

Intriguing.

He narrowed his eyes. 'Should I be worried here? Do you have an insanely jealous lover who's about to storm over and demand I step outside or something? Only you seem to be arguing with yourself about the wisdom of speaking to me.'

She let out a deep guttural laugh, the dirty carnal suggestion of it playing along his senses, making something fizz and tickle deep in his throat.

He swallowed hard.

'I'm freshly out of a disastrous fling with someone who couldn't care less about me, actually. I seem to have a knack for choosing losers and users.' She swayed in towards him. 'What is it about me that screams *sucker,* do you think, Tristan?'

He knew he shouldn't articulate what had just flitted through his mind, but there was something about her beleaguered expression that made it impossible to resist.

'From where I'm standing, *sucker* is a word full of possibilities.' His gaze dropped to that smooth, curvy pout of hers as it twisted into a smile and he saw her shift in her heels as she twigged exactly what he was insinuating.

Lu turned away from his gaze and took another hefty swig of her wine before placing the glass carefully back onto the bar, her fingertips catching the stem at the last second so that it spun and rocked for a moment before settling down to its former inanimate state. The spots of colour on her cheeks flared further outwards.

Was she nervous? Or excited by the idea?

He realised with uncomfortable certainty that he hoped it was the latter.

Whoa, boy. Put the brakes on that impulse.

Chatting to a woman in a bar was one thing, but taking it further wasn't on the agenda right now.

Was it?

'You celebrating something?' he said, nodding towards the huddle of women at the table she'd just vacated in an attempt to take the charged atmosphere down a notch or two.

'A friend's birthday. We both work round the corner so this is our after-work local.' Something troubling seemed to occur to her and she frowned and picked up her glass again, taking another large gulp of wine. After giving herself a little shake, she flashed him a wide smile.

'How about you? What are you doing here all on your lonesome?' She made another move towards him, drawing herself up to her full height and putting out an arm to casually lean on the bar, bringing her tantalising floral fragrance with her.

He drew in a deep lungful of her heady scent and

smiled down at her. 'I ducked in here to avoid being mauled by a woman with a hungry look in her eyes.'

She looked at him steadily. 'She fancied a slice of you, did she?'

'I got that impression, yes.'

'And you didn't feel like being her Tristan Topping tonight?'

He laughed. 'Or any other night.'

She swallowed and stared somewhere to the left side of his head before flicking her gaze back to his. There was a flash of something he couldn't quite pin down in those baby-blues.

She was one contrary lady. One minute cool and assertive, buying him a drink, the next uncertain and wary.

He'd not come across someone like Lu for a very long time. Since splitting with Marcy he'd only seemed to meet women who had formed hard, flawless shells around themselves, who gave him a perfectly polished response every time—who thought they were giving him what he wanted, when actually he was repelled by their phoniness.

But this woman had something about her that he couldn't bear to step away from just yet.

She was too damn interesting.

Pull yourself together, you lunatic.

Lula turned away from the disconcertingly gorgeous man in front of her and glanced over to where her party sat laughing at something Emily had said. Her friend was standing and waving her arms around in an approximation of sexual fervour in her typical crowd-pleasing style.

Em would know exactly what to say to a guy like

this, and she certainly wouldn't have made a total fool of herself by coughing all over him.

He'd taken her by surprise, rocking up to the bar before she could formulate a plan about how best to approach him, and she'd been totally unprepared for the immediate visceral effect he'd had on her.

He wasn't the type of man she'd usually go for—he was scarily charismatic and his powerful virility and snappy smartness gave her the jitters. He was just so chiselled and *smooth*-looking with his Roman nose and intelligent, rich brown eyes that sparked with amusement behind a pair of those trendy rectangular-framed 'invisible' glasses.

He was totally *business*.

She had a mad urge to mess with his neatly swept back hair, to ruffle him up a bit and see the raw side of the man concealed beneath the sharply tailored suit.

Blood throbbed through her veins as she entertained the impulse.

She felt slightly bad about not correcting him when he'd asked if her name was short for Louise, but it had occurred to her that she could pretend to be someone else entirely tonight and it wouldn't matter a jot. She'd never see him again, so why not fully step into the persona she wanted to project? A fake name was a great way to do that, and it wasn't as if anyone was going to get hurt.

Looking back at him, she realised he was frowning down at her as if trying to figure out what the heck was going through her head. He must think she was a total simpleton, first rambling on about her failed relationships, then suggesting he wasn't a real man and now staring around like a vacant airhead.

Gah.

After taking one more bolstering swig of wine, she turned to regain eye contact and gave him her most seductive smile.

'So what made you pick this particular pub for a refuge from the man-eater?' she asked.

He shrugged and twisted his beer bottle between his fingers. 'I'm staying in the hotel across the road and this looked like a suitably dark and shady place to hide.'

'So you don't live in London?' That was good. It meant they were unlikely to ever bump into each other again.

Unless they wanted to?

That's not on the agenda tonight, Lula, get a grip.

Tristan shook his head and frowned. 'I'm based in Edinburgh.'

'I've never been there. I hear it's a really cool place.'

'It is.'

'So what brings you this far south?' she asked.

'Business. I had a meeting in Canary Wharf today and I have something to do for my father tomorrow.' His voice had become rougher, as if he was uncomfortable—or maybe bored—talking about it.

Lula nodded and smiled, attempting to hide her anxiety. Her radio training told her she needed to latch onto a more interesting topic of conversation or she was going to lose him.

'So is it true that men who wear glasses make better lovers?' She cringed inside, amazed at the guff that came out of her mouth in times of stress.

He let out a startled guffaw. 'That's not one I've heard before, but since I fit firmly into that category I'm going to say *yes*.'

She smiled, happy not to have been slapped down

and amazed to feel the atmosphere begin to zing between them again.

May as well go with it.

'I think it has something to do with losing one of your senses when you take your glasses off—your eyesight, obviously, in this instance—which makes you work harder with your sense of touch.'

He dipped his head in mirth. 'That sounds like a load of gobbledegook to me, but I'm willing to go with it if it makes you believe I'll be better in bed than my non-bespectacled rivals.'

'Oh, I have no doubt you are,' Lu said, the heat in her cheeks intensifying as she struggled to maintain flirty eye contact.

Out of the corner of her eye she noticed Emily making her way over to where they stood at the bar and primed herself for whatever might happen next.

Everything about her friend shouted *Look at me!,* from her abundance of blonde-tipped, chocolate-coloured curls and large golden eyes to her curvy statuesque figure.

She *struck* people.

And she made things happen—it was what made her such a successful TV presenter. Normally Lula loved that about her, but right now she needed to be allowed to handle this situation with Tristan without Em's dominating personality muscling in.

'So, Lu, I guess you're not coming to the next pub with us then?' Emily said as she approached, widening her eyes and unsubtly twitching her head towards Tristan.

'Er, no. I don't think so,' Lula said, hoping her face didn't look as flushed as it felt.

Emily nodded, narrowing her eyes at Tristan. 'Hold

this for me, will you?' she said, thrusting her drink at him.

He took it from her and watched in apparent amusement as she rummaged in her bag for something.

'Do me a favour, take a sip of that and tell me if you think it's gin or vodka they've put in there. I think it's gin, but the barman swears it's vodka,' Emily said, her head still in her bag.

Tristan took a small sip. 'Definitely not gin,' he said.

Em pulled her phone out of her bag and took a quick snap of Tristan with the camera on it. Before he had chance to ask her what she was doing, she wrapped a tissue around her hand and took her glass from him.

'Thanks. Right, well, you look after my friend here, because if you attempt anything she doesn't like I have your picture, fingerprints and DNA and I will not hesitate to hand them over to the police. Consider yourself warned.'

'Jeez, Emily, leave the poor guy alone,' Lula said, rolling her eyes at her friend, hoping to God Tristan would see the funny side. When she turned to give him an apologetic smile she was relieved to find he was smiling, albeit in a rather bemused way.

'Okay, I'm backing away now,' Emily sang out. 'I'll leave you in Lu's capable hands,' she said, giving Tristan a salacious wink.

Lula's insides shrivelled in mortification.

Leaning in, Emily gave her a tight hug, whispering, 'You *go,* girl. Show this guy who's boss,' into Lu's ear before flashing them both a wicked grin and hurrying off.

CHAPTER TWO

HE STAYED TALKING with her for another hour after her crazy friend had left, enjoying her company more and more as she seemed to relax with him.

They chatted about everything and nothing; he teased her about her love of nineties music, which she countered by turning her nose up at his obsession with trad jazz. They discussed their favourite books from childhood, his passion for following Formula One racing and her seemingly encyclopaedic knowledge of art-house films.

Despite her reluctance to leave with her friends, Tristan had a strong suspicion that picking up random guys in a pub wasn't Lu's usual modus operandi. There was something too reserved about her to make him believe she did this kind of thing on a regular basis. He loved the fact she was clearly making a special effort for him—he hadn't felt that wanted in a while—but unfortunately it pointed towards the possibility that she'd expect more from this encounter than he was able to give.

She was a sexy and engaging woman and he could imagine she'd be incredible in bed but he probably shouldn't push for anything to happen between them.

He didn't do one-night stands. And he didn't need any complications while he was here. As soon as this radio station mess was resolved he'd be on the first plane back to Edinburgh—back to running the family business that his father had now totally lost interest in.

He drained the last of his third bottle of beer. 'I should probably go,' he said gently.

The look of bewildered disappointment, which she quickly forced into an unconcerned smile, made his heart do a slow dive. She clearly didn't want this encounter to end and, if he was *totally* honest, neither did he.

'No problem,' she said, knocking back the last of her wine and placing the glass onto the bar.

He noticed, with a jolt of surprise, that her hand seemed to be trembling.

'I really should get going too. Things to do tomorrow.' She gave him a false bright smile.

'Are you going to catch up with your friends?'

'Nah. I don't think I should drink any more.'

He nodded. 'Very sensible.'

Huffing out a laugh, she swept her hand through her heavy blunt-cut fringe. 'That's me, Level-headed *Louise*.' She slung her bag across her shoulder and straightened her top. Looking back up at him, she cracked a rueful smile. 'I'll walk out with you.'

They exited into the cool spring London air, the fume-filled, peppery scents of the city twanging at his senses.

He was painfully aware of her there next to him and acutely conscious that once she walked away the chances of ever seeing her again were practically non-existent. It seemed such a pity when there was such intense chemistry between them.

They came to a stop outside the pub and he put a hand onto her shoulder, feeling the silky material of her top slip beneath his fingers. Her skin was warm beneath his touch and he wanted to leave it there, revelling in the delicate heat of her for a while longer.

She looked up at him questioningly, her bright, open gaze drawing him in deeper. He was utterly mesmerised by the sweet, vulnerable expression on her face.

Neither of them moved as they gazed into each other's eyes, caught in an inexplicable connective tension that made it impossible for him to turn away from her. This had never happened to him before—this strange, undeniable pull—and it made him weirdly nervous.

He finally found his voice. 'Look, Lu, I think you're a very attractive woman and far be it from me to deny you the chance to find out whether your theory about men with glasses is correct, but I should probably do the gentlemanly thing and flag you down a cab.'

'Yeah, that would be the *sensible* thing to do,' she murmured in that tormenting voice of hers, still looking him dead in the eye.

Something tugged low and hard, deep in his pelvis. Ah, boy, it was going to be painfully difficult to walk away from her and go back to his cold, empty hotel room when she was looking at him like that. He wanted to gather her in to him and kiss the life out of her. To lose himself in her warmth, to forget about all the responsibilities that waited for his attention in the real world.

'I've really enjoyed meeting you tonight,' he said, his voice coming out husky and rough.

Her smile was faltering. 'It was lovely to meet you too.' Putting both hands on his chest, she pressed them into him, as if attempting to osmose her sincerity, digging her fingertips gently into his pecs.

His body gave a disturbing throb as everything from

his taste buds to the soles of his feet responded to her. Taking a deep breath and putting his hands over the top of hers, he tilted his head in a show of regret. 'In another universe we'd have an amazing night together.'

She pinched her eyebrows together, her voluptuous mouth turning down at the corners, and took her hands away, dropping them to her sides.

The loss of her touch disturbed him more than it should have.

'You don't have a girlfriend, do you? Or a *wife*?' The idea seemed to horrify her. It horrified him too. He was never getting married. Not when he'd repeatedly seen how miserable it could make you.

Shaking his head, he gave Lu an amused smile. 'Neither. But I have a lot of work to do tonight.' It sounded so pathetic when he said it out loud. Was he really going to work instead of spending more time with this fascinating, capricious woman?

He took a breath, aware she was looking at him with justifiable scepticism. 'The thing is, I'm only here in London—' But he didn't get to finish his sentence because she reached up to lay one of her small, cool hands against his neck and draw his head down to her lush, waiting mouth.

Her lips were warm and soft against his and he closed his eyes reflexively, drinking in the erotic intimacy of her touch. Barely a second later she drew back and he blinked his eyes open and stared at her, taking in her own surprise at the unexpectedly audacious action.

'I just needed to do that,' she whispered in that taunting voice of hers.

All the arguments that had previously filtered through his mind evaporated into the sultry night air along with his resolve as he lost the tenuous grip on his control. Moving quickly towards her, he recaptured her soft, wine-scented mouth with his.

She let out a deep, low moan in the back of her throat, the sexy desperation of it nearly undoing him and he darted his tongue into her mouth, tasting the sweetness of her.

He stopped her from stumbling backwards by putting his hands on her hips and pulling her roughly towards him, pressing their bodies close together. She responded by sliding her arms around his waist and kissing him back with a ferocity that made his whole body tighten with lust.

A pulse-quickening notion of what could happen if they didn't stop this ran through his head: him leading her back to his hotel across the road, them kissing fiercely in the elevator as they travelled up to the fourth floor, stumbling into his room, already tugging each other's clothes off as they tried to make it to the bed before they lost all control and ended up in a sweaty, writhing mess on the floor.

He could see it all unfold—practically taste it—but he shouldn't let that happen.

Should he?

She slipped her hands under his jacket and dragged her nails down his back, leaving tingling lines of sensation across his skin.

His body responded immediately and she gasped against his mouth as his arousal made itself known between the press of their bodies.

She ground herself harder against him, her soft, flowery scent pummelling his senses, and he wondered hazily *why* exactly he thought it was a good idea to stop this. Work and a failed relationship weren't decent enough excuses to ruin a perfectly good opportunity for one night of pleasure with a beautiful stranger; a stranger currently intent on seducing him with her cool wandering hands and small muffled moans of pleasure.

He could really use some light relief from the soberness of his life right now.

Sod it. He wanted this. She clearly wanted this. It was happening.

Lula barely took in the luxury of her surroundings as Tristan guided her into his hotel room, continuing the mind-blowing kiss they'd been unable to resist in the elevator on their way up there.

She could hardly believe this was happening, but she was mightily glad it was. The alcohol had given her wings and when he'd looked at her with such heat in his eyes she'd not been able to stop herself from reaching up and kissing him.

She'd never felt so attractive, so *desired* before and the thought of walking away from that feeling had been unimaginable.

Clearly it had been for him too, because he'd responded immediately to her brazen gesture, dragging her against his rock-hard body in a possessive gesture that made her feel so wanted.

That was the moment that undid her—when every other thought and consideration flew right out of her head and all her nerves and reticence disappeared in a puff of lust.

There was something so freeing about letting herself go with him—about not worrying what he thought of her as she ran her hands all over his body, or made the low breathy sounds that came from deep within her throat.

For the first time in a long time she felt empowered and sexy and *alive*.

She *needed* this right now. So badly.

Raising her arms, she let him drag her top up over her head and drop it on the floor by their feet, moving swiftly round to fiddle with the clasp of her bra until it pinged loose and he discarded that too.

'You have magnificent breasts, Louise,' he growled, dropping to his knees and taking one of her nipples into his mouth, tugging on it gently with his teeth before swirling his tongue around the swollen areola.

She only just stopped herself from correcting him on her name as sensational pleasure ripped through her body, centring where his mouth locked against her breast, his lips and teeth teasing at her skin.

Louise *was* her name tonight. Louise was a beguiling, sexually assertive woman she didn't recognise, but tonight she was going to possess her body and mind for her own pure, selfish pleasure.

Skimming his hands round from where they rested on her hips, Tristan fiddled with the button of her jeans until they popped open and he was able to ease down the zip and slide the heavy material down her legs to the floor. He helped her step out of her heels, looking up and flashing her such a sensual smile that her whole body gave a throb of longing.

Grasping his head in her hands, she drew him upwards, back to standing so she could kiss him hard. She needed to even things up here, to give as well as take, before she lost her nerve.

'I want to feel you—against me,' she muttered against his mouth.

She felt him smile, and the next second she was left gaping in a chasm of cool air as he stepped back to yank off his tie, then pull his shirt—still buttoned—over his head.

Dropping them onto the floor, he gave her a teasing come-hither look and she stepped forwards to put the palms of her trembling hands against the amazing honed plane of his chest.

Her breath caught in her throat as she fully took in the hard contours of his body.

He *definitely* worked out.

'I've never seen a six-pack in real life before,' she said, glancing up at him and attempting to smile without looking like a total goof.

He was staring down at her, the heat and intensity of his arousal plain in his eyes.

Her stomach did a disconcerting swoop.

'Come here.' He dragged her against him and their bodies clashed and melded together, the heat of his bleeding into hers in glorious waves.

Then his mouth was hot and hard on hers again, his tongue darting into her mouth, tickling her sensitised lips and sweeping her teeth, probing and pushing, deeper and more insistently than before.

She wanted that tongue on her skin. Everywhere.

But first she was going to give him a taste of his own delicious medicine.

It took a moment of fumbling before she managed to open the clasp of his trousers, but then she was free to slide them down his muscular legs. He toed off his shoes and she watched him quickly discard the rest of his clothes until he towered over her totally naked, looking like some biologically perfect specimen of man.

His hair was mussed now where she'd run her hands through it and his glasses glinted in the soft light of the lamp he'd left on. There was something obscenely hot about him wearing only a pair of glasses and a grin and she shivered in lust-fuelled anticipation.

Pushing him against the wall, she ran her hands all over the hard contours of his chest, taking in the defined lines of his muscles and the contrasting soft sleekness of his skin. The naked power of him made her faintly jittery, but she knew she was safe with him.

She trusted him and he appeared to trust her.

The fact he was letting her push him around like this was a huge boost to her confidence. He wasn't just taking what he wanted; he was waiting to see what she gave him.

Something about that made her intensely happy. She'd never experienced this feeling of sexual control with a man before and because he was allowing her to take the lead, her nerves had now completely vanished.

It was encouraging and very, *very* hot.

Sliding her hand down his body, she found his hard shaft hovering against his belly and tickled her fingertips over the head, smiling to herself as she heard his sharp intake of breath. Wrapping her hand around him, she moved it against him in slow, fluid strokes, dropping her head at the same time to place soft, teasing kisses against his solid chest, twisting her tongue against his nipples then stretching up to lick the hard lines of his collarbone and dip into the hollows of his neck.

His skin was the perfect mixture of sweet and salty and her mouth watered in response to the dual tang as she swept her tongue over him.

'I want to eat you up, you're so delicious,' she murmured against his skin and felt his chest expand and contract as he laughed quietly.

She spent some time exploring his broad torso with her lips and tongue, all the while keeping up a steady rhythm with her hand. Her breath came hot and fast, leaving a faint mist of moisture on his skin where she played her mouth against him. She could hear his breathing, deep and ragged in his chest as she worked him over.

'Lu…' His voice came out as a ragged plea.

'Yes?' Her own sounded just as distorted.

'I can't take much more of this kind of manhandling. You're gonna have to stop if you don't want this to be over too soon.'

'Okay…' she whispered, tightening her hand around him for one last teasing squeeze.

Half groaning, half laughing, Tristan slid his hands under her buttocks and lifted her against him, the hardness of his arousal pressing with excruciating pleasure against the zingy heat between her legs as he carried her over to the king-sized bed.

Lowering her onto it, he bent to kiss her mouth hard before making his way south, roaming over the highly stimulated skin of her breasts again—lingering there for a minute until she thought she might come just from the attention he was giving them—before moving lower.

Her body throbbed in anticipation as he slid her knickers down her legs, then stooped to run his tongue around the exposed triangle between her thighs, skimming the most sensitive parts of her until she almost screamed with the need for him to touch and lick here *there*.

When he eventually did, it was as if he'd zapped her with a live wire of pure pleasure and instinctively she raised her hips off the bed to press herself harder against him.

Never had she felt so on the edge of control. And it felt *goooood*.

He used gentle, sweeping strokes on her, over and over bringing her closer, exquisitely closer to the edge of orgasm. But she wanted more.

What would Louise say to get what she wanted?

'I want you inside me,' she whispered, hoping she'd said it loudly enough for him to hear. He stopped what he was doing and moved up the bed, trailing kisses along her skin, nipping once at each nipple before kissing her full on the mouth again.

She needed her control back. Right now.

'On your back,' she demanded, twisting out from under him and shoving against one shoulder to tip him into the position she wanted him.

He landed on his back and raised an amused eyebrow at her, a faint smile playing around his mouth.

'Who'd have thought someone so petite could be so domineering,' he said, sliding a hand into her hair to draw her mouth down to his.

'Small but determined, that's me,' she said, once she'd finished kissing him.

'I can see that.' The look in his eyes told her he was totally fine with it too.

'Wait here,' she said, backing off the bed and hurrying over to where her clothes lay on the other side of the room.

Jeez, the suite was enormous. It must be costing a few bob to stay here. He must be into some serious business to afford it.

Pushing the errant thought out of her mind, she located her handbag and rummaged in one of the inside pockets, pulling out tissues, café loyalty cards and hair bobbles until she found what she was looking for.

Turning back to the bed, she saw Tristan had propped

himself up on his elbows and was watching her with interest. She waved her loot in the air in a show of triumph.

'You carry your own condoms?'

She shrugged, suddenly painfully conscious of how it might look. 'Sure, why not? It's just as much my responsibility as yours,' she mumbled.

Her spirits rose as he gave her an impressed look and nodded slowly. 'I'm beginning to like you, Louise,' he said, and she very nearly corrected him again.

No, Lula, stay in character.

Climbing back onto the bed, she straddled his legs and slid her way back up his body, dragging her nipples against his shins, over his knees and thighs, then cupping her breasts together with one hand to trap the hard length of his shaft between them. He groaned as she slid him back and forth between the soft cushions, propping herself up on one arm and lazily running her tongue over the peaks and troughs of his abs at the same time.

She paused what she was doing as he slid his hands into her hair and began to stroke his fingers gently against her scalp in rhythm with the movement.

It was a beautifully intimate thing for him to do and an unexpected swell of emotion expanded in her chest.

Most of her sexual encounters had been swift and to the point. No one had ever touched and stroked her the way Tristan did. As if she was something to treasure and worship.

He must have thought she didn't like what he was doing because he took his hands away and when she looked up she saw he'd stretched his arms above his head and was pressing his hands against the headboard.

She wanted to tell him she'd liked how he made her

feel, but she didn't know how to say it without it sounding cheesy or, even worse, needy. And, anyway, it would have been a total mood-breaker to start discussing feelings at that precise moment. She wasn't there to *talk*.

Moving her way up his body, she positioned herself so she was sitting on the tops of his thighs, trapping him beneath her.

He looked up at her and gave her a slow smile. 'I like looking at you, sitting there all sexy and self-assured.'

The comment gave her a little zing of anxiety in her chest. She didn't want him to be focused on her; she wanted him concentrating on his own pleasure. Reaching forward, she plucked his glasses off his nose and put them carefully on the nightstand next to the bed.

He groaned in grumpy frustration. 'I can't see you now.'

'That's the idea. You're going to have to feel me instead,' she said, tearing open the condom wrapper.

He groaned again, but this time it was filled with pure hunger.

She took a moment to slide the latex over him, enjoying his little growls of pleasure as she did so.

Moving up on her knees, she positioned herself above him, fitting the tip of him inside her. She smiled as she heard his deep intake of breath and he gripped the headboard harder. Slowly, carefully, she lowered herself onto him, relishing the exquisite stretch and pressure as he filled her. She was so keyed up, it felt as though a million nerve-endings had come alive and were dancing with joy inside her.

They fitted together perfectly, the length of him hitting her deep inside, and she couldn't stop herself from moving straight away, savouring the ebb and flow of sensation as she pressed deep, then pulled up and almost off him again.

'Whoa, whoa, whoa…' Tristan muttered, as she continued to move and leant back to put a hand on each of his thighs, letting her hair cascade down her back.

She felt him buck beneath her and increased her speed, rocking her pelvis back and forth, delighting in the delicious friction inside her.

Tipping her head back to look at him, she saw him lick the fingers of one hand then slide it between her legs, pressing on her sensitive nub and sending a whole new riot of sensation through her.

Releasing her grip on his legs, she leaned forwards into the pressure of his caress and picked up the pace, feeling the beginnings of an orgasm as it teased her body, shimmering like a halo of pleasure on the horizon.

The dual sensations intensified as she rode him and lost herself in the pure hedonism of the moment. Delicious pressure built and built until she thought she might go crazy with the need for release and finally the feeling broke and she flew over the edge, plummeting into a deep, dark cavern of euphoria, pinpricks of light exploding behind her eyes.

It took a good few moments for her blissed-out state to dispel enough for her to rise from where she'd slumped against Tristan's chest but, when she did, she saw he was giving her the most wickedly delighted smirk.

'It sounded like you enjoyed that,' he said.

'I might have found it pleasingly uplifting,' she replied, unable to keep the laughter out of her voice.

'I'm relieved I didn't let my bespectacled brothers down.'

'No, no, I can safely say they'd be more than satisfied with your sterling performance,' she said, shifting a little, only to discover how hard he still was inside her.

He let out a muffled curse and clenched his fists above his head. 'Please tell me you're not going to leave me like this.'

'You really think I'd be that cruel,' she said, shifting her hips again to restart the slip-slide motion, conjuring up wonderful aftershocks from her orgasm.

His breath rasped in his throat as they moved faster together and she allowed him to set the pace this time, matching his thrusts as he found his rhythm.

Leaning forwards, she pressed her hands onto his shoulders to hold him against the bed—the sheen of sweat on his skin causing her grip to slip a little—and continued to move with him, squeezing him inside her on the upstroke. She could feel his muscles quivering beneath her touch and he bucked his hips, his breathing growing more and more ragged until he finally let out a low groan of pleasure, his brow furrowing hard in concentrated pleasure as he came inside her.

It was a truly beautiful sight.

She'd done that to him. *She'd* made this gorgeous, ridiculously sexy man lose his mind like that.

They *worked* together.

Something she could only describe as a mind orgasm flooded through her head at the thought of it.

She stayed on top of him until his breathing quietened and he opened his eyes again and smiled at her.

'Well, Louise, I have to admit I'm very grateful you coughed all over me tonight.' He placed a hand on her hip and stroked his fingertips up and down, tickling the line of her spine.

Despite her wave of discomfort at him not using her

real name, her body still gave a delicious shiver in response to his touch.

'Just think,' he continued, an eyebrow raised. 'If you hadn't we might have both been alone in our separate beds right now instead of enjoying the warm afterglow of down and dirty sex together.'

Levering herself off him, she collapsed onto the bed, trying not to worry about how wobbly she felt.

The slow, sad pull of loneliness that had bugged her recently had no business raising its ugly head right now. There was no room for anything other than sexual satisfaction at this precise moment.

He turned to look at her and the jubilant expression on his face made her heart turn over.

Down, girl.

'Seriously, that was incredible. It was exactly what I needed,' he said, rubbing a hand over his eyes, then flopping it down onto the bed next to him, a wide, satisfied grin splashed across his face.

She took a deep controlling breath, suddenly terrified by a disorientating muddle of thoughts and feelings that hurtled through her head.

Surely the end of a one-night stand wasn't supposed to feel like this—so...melancholy. She should be bouncing out of there with a spring in her step, not mooching about like a lost puppy, desperate for more attention.

From out of nowhere, the nervy fear about the meeting in the morning came back to hit her with full force in the chest.

What the hell was she doing?

She should get out of there. Right now.

'Okay, well, good,' she said shakily, sitting up and swinging her legs over the bed. 'I'm gonna get going.'

She felt the bed dip behind her as he rolled onto his side and grabbed his glasses off the nightstand.

'You're leaving? Right now?'

'I have things to do tomorrow.' She couldn't look at him in case he saw the bewildering swirl of emotion she was battling to hide.

She couldn't stay, not if she had any chance of staying sane.

And, anyway, Tristan would probably freak out if she started acting like this was anything other than a one-night stand.

Better to cut her losses and go now.

She jumped up off the bed and went over to where their clothes lay in a muddled heap on the floor. Flinging his things out of the way, she located all of hers and pulled them on quickly, intensely aware of his gaze on her back.

'What? I gave you such an incredible orgasm there's no point in even trying to top it?' His tone was jokey, but she detected a faintly indignant twang.

She laughed despite herself. 'I'll certainly never forget it.' She turned back to look at him and took a step towards where he now sat on the edge of the bed, keeping a couple of feet between them. Maintaining a safe distance from that tantalising body of his. 'But I get the feeling you wouldn't be interested in a sleepover.'

'Well, no—'

'And, to be honest, I'm not a good bedfellow anyway. I move around a lot. And I steal the sheets. I'd keep you awake and you'd regret even suggesting it.'

He was frowning now, clearly baffled by her word vomit.

'It's okay, Louise, I wasn't suggesting that.'

She sighed and rubbed a hand over her forehead,

feeling downright sleazy now for not telling him her real name. 'It's been fun, Tristan. *Really* good fun, but I think it's best if I don't hang around.'

Argh, how were you meant to do this kind of thing without sounding like a prude or a heinous bitch?

Tristan stood up and caught hold of Lu's arm as she turned to go. 'Hey, wait.' Drawing her towards him, he bent to kiss her again for the last time, attempting to make it a kiss she'd never forget.

The groan she gave in the back of her throat made him think he'd succeeded.

He felt discombobulated by her sudden need to depart and wanted to slow her down, keep her for a bit longer, even if it was only for one extra minute.

Breaking away, she gave him a look of pure regret. 'I'm not going to be able to leave if you keep doing things like that.'

He smiled. 'That's the idea.'

Her gaze flitted to the floor and his stomach sank as he realised he'd said the wrong thing. This was a one-night-only thing. That was all he'd thought he wanted—until he'd found how sexually explosive they were together. Now he wanted to suggest he stayed in London for an extra day so they could spend one more night together—one very *long* night—to give them the chance to explore exactly how much more fun they could conjure up between them.

Letting her go now seemed like such a travesty.

Apparently Lu didn't share his view.

She stepped forwards to give him one last soft kiss on the lips, then turned and walked swiftly away, closing the door quietly behind her.

And then she was gone.

After showering, he stared at himself in the bathroom mirror, trying to ignore the way his body seemed desperate for more of Lu's intensive attention. His eyes looked brighter than normal and his skin was flushed and glowing. That was what a good, hard bout of amazing sex did to you. It made you look and feel alive. Something he'd been missing for a while now.

He'd been surprised by how much he'd loved the way Lu had taken control. Normally he was the one leading things in the bedroom—it had never occurred to him not to—and he'd been pleasantly surprised by just how much he'd liked it when she took over. And by how willing he was to trust her. Maybe it was because he had to be responsible in every other part of his life; handing control over to someone else for a change had been liberating.

Going back into the bedroom, he gathered up his clothes from the floor. His gaze caught on something the size and shape of a credit card as it fell out from the folds of his shirt. He scooped it up and looked at it. It was a driver's licence. Louise must have dropped it out of her bag when she went looking for condoms. A feeling of euphoria rose in his chest. He might have just found a reason to contact her again.

Turning it over, he glanced quickly at the cute picture of Lu before reading the name underneath it.

Tallulah Lazenby.

His whole body went cold as the name sank into his brain. Why was it so familiar? And why was he experiencing this sick, sinking feeling?

Grabbing his laptop, he opened up the mail from his father giving him the details for the meeting at the radio station tomorrow. He scanned the text until his eyes alighted on the name of the woman his father wanted to fire.

Tallulah Lazenby.

She'd told him her name was Louise.

She'd lied to him.

His mind flitted back to all the moments that evening where she'd seemed to correct herself or change up her performance with him.

She'd known who he was all along—deliberately latching onto him and seducing him, perhaps hoping he'd think twice before firing her from her job.

He'd been played for a fool. Again.

Flinging the card across the room, he flopped down onto the bed, furious with himself for being stupid enough to think this had been one of those genuinely serendipitous events.

Hot humiliation washed through him, followed by icy anger. It felt just as bad as when he'd found out Marcy had been cheating on him.

No. Worse.

This had been a deliberate plan to manipulate him.

That was why she'd choked when they'd first met; she must have seen a picture of him somewhere. His father had been known to include photos of his family members in his press releases if he thought it would benefit his businesses—to promote himself as a trustworthy employer with family values. What a joke that was.

And he'd told her his name. He had a sudden memory flash of what he'd *thought* was her deciding whether to talk to him or not. She must have been deciding how best to get one over on him.

Damn it. How had he allowed himself to be taken for such a fool?

Pulling the sheet over him in frustration, he attempted to settle his still frustratingly aroused body into a comfortable sleeping position.

One thing was for sure, it was going to be a very *interesting* meeting tomorrow.

CHAPTER THREE

THE NEXT MORNING, Lula held her thumping head in her hands as her bus made slow progress towards Covent Garden.

How could she have thought it was a good idea to have such a wild night when she had to go into work this morning and defend herself against King Dong Jez?

Clearly something had snapped in her tiny, overwrought brain.

Not that she exactly regretted her time spent with Tristan.

A warm wave of pleasure swept through her body as she remembered how great he'd tasted, all musky and earthy and sweet. Like salted caramel and strong coffee and sex. Delicious. Her taste buds tingled in response to the sensory memory. He'd smelt amazing too, like fresh linen and spicy shaving gel and cleanness.

If only she could bottle his amazing scent and market it, it'd probably sell out in minutes and make her a fortune. She'd never need to work again.

Not that she did it for the money. Ever since she'd discovered the buzz of pride and sense of accomplishment she got from hosting a radio show she'd been totally focused on getting to where she was today.

She couldn't have this job snatched away from her now; it would break her heart.

Alighting from the bus, she put her sunglasses on to protect her poor tired eyes against the bright spring sunshine and shoved her way through the crowded shopping streets of Covent Garden.

After some expert ducking and dodging, she made it to the quieter end where the radio station was housed on the top floor of an old converted red-brick warehouse. Climbing the innumerable stairs, she felt her heart thudding against her ribcage in protest at the intense cardio workout. She wanted to go home, put her head under her pillow and blot out the rest of the day, but she knew she had to pull up her big girl pants and face whatever was in store for her today.

There was no running away from this mess.

Her stomach rumbled and flipped over as she walked into the sharply stylish, über contemporary reception area, which always smelled wonderfully of fresh coffee and the amazing Danish pastries that Flora the Receptionist kept strictly for visitors to the station.

She remembered with regret how she hadn't even had time to grab breakfast after sleeping through her alarm and having to scramble into the shower then throw on the first set of smart clothes that came to hand. There hadn't even been time for pain relief—she'd desperately rifled through the medicine cupboard only to find she was out of paracetamol—so now she was going to have to sit through her meeting with a churning stomach and a head that felt as if someone was banging a thousand tiny hammers against it.

As she was standing there contemplating her fate, one of the broadcast assistants walked past her into reception carrying what smelled like a hot bacon sandwich and she nearly fell to her knees with need.

'Claire? I will love you for ever and have your darling babies if you let me buy that from you,' she gasped, her eyes glued to the potential lifeline in Claire's hand.

'Sorry, Lula, no can do.' Claire smiled apologetically. 'This is for the Big Cheese that's here for your meeting. He's been prowling round the station like a disgruntled tiger since he got here and I daren't be much longer or he might bite my head off and eat that instead.'

Ugh! This morning got worse and worse. Now it looked as if she was going to have to sit in a room and watch her bad-tempered judge and juror chomp his way through breakfast nectar while her own stomach shrivelled to nothing—right before she was unceremoniously fired.

'God, he sounds like a monster,' she muttered, looking at Claire beseechingly, hoping for some little titbit to prepare her for what lay in wait behind the conference room door.

'He probably just got out of bed the wrong side today,' Claire said, shrugging one shoulder. She leaned in closer to Lula and dropped her voice. 'He's younger than I was expecting and much better-looking.' From the twinkle in her eye, Lula could tell Claire was a little awestruck.

'I thought he was in his sixties? Jez told me their fathers are friends from their University days,' Lula said, frowning at the inconsistency. She'd never seen Claire swoon over anyone past the age of thirty-five, let alone someone old enough to be her grandfather.

'This guy's his son. The father's on his honeymoon somewhere in deepest Asia so the son's stepped in to take your meeting. He runs the family business up in

Scotland, I think. Didn't you see the mailshot everyone was forwarding around the other month with a picture of the two of them? I thought Flora was going to have an orgasm right there in her chair when she saw it.'

'No, I didn't see that one.' Lula sighed and rubbed a hand over her eyes, not in the mood for joking around when her whole body felt strung out with tension. 'I should have been told someone else was taking the meeting,' she muttered, irritation making her voice croaky.

Bloody Jez. He'd probably kept her in the dark deliberately to back-foot her.

Claire dropped her smile and nodded in agreement. 'That's our illustrious leader for you; not exactly a great disseminator of information.'

'Except when he's being "wronged"; then you can't shut the man up,' Lula stated, not even trying to hide her bitterness.

Claire knew all about Jez and his philandering, manipulative ways and she'd been working on the broadcast assistant's desk when he'd come in and told Lula he was giving her show to Darla.

'Good luck in your meeting,' Claire said, resting a hand gently on Lula's shoulder and giving her a supportive smile.

Lula got the impression a lot of the staff members were on her side, even if most of them hadn't said anything directly to her for fear of word getting back to Jez and losing their jobs too, but the thought gave her a tiny surge of courage.

'Hey, perhaps this guy will give Jez the old heave-ho and step into the breach himself?' Claire added, gazing longingly at the closed conference room door. 'I have to say, despite the crankiness, I wouldn't mind him sticking around here for a bit. Total eye candy.' She wiggled her eyebrows, gave Lula one last smile, then turned and walked off to deliver the food to the man in question.

Lula sighed and rubbed at the corners of her temple where the pain had concentrated. Great. Now she was facing a *sex god* boss with a bacon sandwich. Could things get any worse?

Tristan wasn't exactly at his best and brightest.

After tossing and turning for hours, he'd woken early that morning, his head spinning with dreams about Tallulah, and even pounding away on the running machine in the hotel gym hadn't relieved any of the frustration that still clung to him.

He'd arrived at the radio station at eight-thirty, eager to get this mess wrapped up and back to some real work, expecting to catch Jez straight after he'd finished presenting his Breakfast Show.

Apparently Jez had had other ideas though, skipping out straight after his show finished, leaving word that he had another meeting to attend before he could see Tristan.

It had not improved Tristan's temper. The guy knew how to take liberties, that was for sure.

To pass the time before his meeting with Tallulah, he'd looked round the station and chatted to some of the staff—who seemed friendly and happy with how Jez ran things there—and was now stationed in the migraine-inducing canary-yellow conference room, attempting to answer some emails before she turned up.

He was barely able to concentrate on what he was doing as flashes of the night before kept interrupting his thoughts. Every time he remembered something else she'd said or done to entice him to sleep with her, his frustration levels rose another notch.

She'd totally played him.

Abandoning his emails, he stood up and paced around the room, glancing out of the window to stare blankly towards the thronging streets of Covent Garden below.

The most infuriating thing was that he'd genuinely liked her.

A lot.

Recalling how she'd made him laugh last night gave him a hollow ache in his chest, followed swiftly by a low sensual pull deep in his pelvis as his thoughts moved onto how she'd pushed him against the wall and run her tongue all over him, her cool hands stroking him to fever pitch…

Damn it. He really needed to stop thinking about her in that way. He was supposed to be conducting a serious interview with her in a minute and he needed to keep things professional.

For the sake of his pride, if nothing else.

He ran a hand carefully over his hair, smoothing a few rogue strands back into place, then sat back in his chair, stretching out his tense back and shoulders. He wasn't going to let her get to him again with those pseudo-innocent eyes and soft pouty lips. Or the sweet intoxicating way she smelled. Or the way she moved that spectacular body of hers…

His thoughts were interrupted by one of the staff members bringing in the breakfast he'd requested and placing it reverentially onto the table in front of him.

He smiled at her. 'Thanks.'

Her cautious nod and tentative returning smile made him frown as he watched her leave the room. Perhaps he'd been a bit fierce with them all this morning? He wasn't exactly in the best mood to meet new people. Or maybe they were worried about their own positions here. After all, it looked as though it had been a while since anyone had audited the station—Jez had been pretty much left to his own devices—and, in his experience, the staff didn't like it when new people were introduced to the equation. It usually meant change.

He'd take a look at the accounts as well while he was here, so he could satisfy himself he'd done a thorough job. He hated leaving loose ends.

Looking down at the food he'd ordered, he realised he wasn't actually hungry any more. Pushing it to one side, he checked the time on his phone.

Right on cue, there was a knock on the door and it opened slowly to reveal the woman he'd not stopped thinking about since she'd walked out of his hotel room a few hours earlier.

Tallulah's face was pale in contrast to the dark circles around her eyes and her hair was pulled back into a severe twist, perversely making her seem younger and more vulnerable than the woman he remembered.

He couldn't let that cloud his decision, though. In fact, she'd probably deliberately chosen that look to appeal to his soft side.

He shifted in his chair as his stomach plunged and twisted at the memory of *her* soft side pressed against him.

'Hello, *Tallulah*. Come in.' He gestured towards the seat next to him, keeping his movements firm and steady.

She was staring at him, her eyes wide and her mouth hanging open as though her greeting had caught in her throat.

Was she really going to pretend to be surprised to see him here? Did she have the gall?

'Tristan?' Her voice came out in a breathy whisper and she dipped her chin and cleared her throat, glancing over her shoulder before stepping into the room and closing the door. Turning back, she held out her hands as if she couldn't believe it was him sitting there. 'What—?' She shook her head, conjuring up a stunned smile. 'What are you doing here?'

Apparently she *did* have the gall.

'You're really going to pretend you didn't know who I was last night?'

She frowned, her cute button nose wrinkling in apparent confusion. 'I didn't—'

'You lied to me. You said your name was Louise.'

Colour flooded her cheeks and she parted her lips and let out a sharp huff of breath, doing a great job of looking abashed.

He crossed his arms. 'So what is it? Louise or Tallulah?'

She shifted in those ludicrous heels of hers and cleared her throat again. 'It's Tallulah.' Catching his eye, she gave him a cautious smile. 'I know, with an *awesome* name like Tallulah Lazenby you'd think I'd be taller,' she joked, clearly hoping to draw a smile from him.

When he didn't respond she walked over to where he was sitting, stumbling a little in her heels, and perched on the chair next to him, splaying her hands, which appeared to be trembling, on the table. 'My friends call me Lu or Lula, but it's short for Tallulah—which I only use for my professional persona.'

She stared down at the table. 'I didn't meant to lie to you; I just thought it would be fun to pretend to be someone else for the evening, so I didn't correct you when you called me Louise.'

Her gaze flicked up to meet his. Her eyes were wide and she was doing a damn good impression of looking mortified at being caught out. 'Believe me, I had no idea it was you I was meeting with today. Jez didn't tell me your father couldn't make it.'

That sensuous voice of hers was evoking the deep sexual ache he'd been battling to ignore since she walked in, only increasing his edginess.

Was she telling the truth? He was disturbed by his inability to tell. It wasn't like him to feel this ruffled and he sure as hell didn't like it.

Sighing, he leant back in his chair, away from her stupefying presence. 'To be honest, I don't know what to believe, Tallulah.'

She looked at him as though he was crazy. 'You think I deliberately lied to you?' Her disdain made the hairs on the back of his neck rise and his blood pump faster.

Marcy had acted in exactly the same way towards him once when he'd accused her of cheating on him—months before she finally admitted she had actually done the dirty and was leaving. His gut feeling had been bang on that time.

Perhaps Tallulah realised she'd been rumbled and was trying to brazen it out by appearing outraged by his suggestion in order to force him to back down.

Not going to happen.

'It's quite a coincidence that we met last night, though. And that you were so keen to sleep with me.'

Her face flushed bright red, but she still managed to give him an are-you-for-real? look. 'I seem to remember you being just as *keen* on the idea.'

He stared back, maintaining cool eye contact. Her

gaze slid away from his and he felt validated by her retreat.

Gotcha.

'Anyway,' she muttered, 'you know what they say: life *is* stranger than fiction.' Her gaze moved to the bacon sandwich on the table next to her and he caught the flash of longing on her face, before she carefully blanked her expression.

'You hungry?' he asked, motioning towards his food. He wondered whether she'd have the balls to try and take his food as well as his pride.

She frowned and glanced up at him, her gaze raking his face for signs of a trap. 'Why? Are you offering me your breakfast?' she asked, clearly suspecting he'd set a booby trap and she'd be ejected straight out of the building if she made so much as a move towards it.

He felt the corner of his mouth twitch into an involuntary smile and had to fight to pull back his stern expression. He shrugged. 'If you want it. Judging by the size of those glasses of wine you downed and the way you exerted yourself last night, I'm guessing you probably need it right about now.'

She leaned forwards in her chair, her eyebrows pinched together and her gaze steady. 'I don't normally do things like that, you know. It was only because it was Laura's birthday and I promised to go and I hate letting people down when I've promised something.'

'Even though you had this meeting today?'

She sighed and sat back, turning to stare out of the window. 'I know, it was unprofessional, but I was nervous about today and then I met you and couldn't drag myself away.' Her gaze flitted back to his and Tristan could have sworn her pupils dilated.

She reached out a hand towards him, but he drew

away quickly. The last thing he needed was for her to touch him when his whole body ached to pull her out of that chair and into his lap. She was clearly trying to use the connection she'd forged with him last night to get herself out of trouble and he needed to be careful.

He crossed his arms against his chest in a show of defensiveness and nodded again to the food in front of her.

'If you want it, it's yours, Tallulah. Go ahead. *Help yourself.*'

'You like your power games, don't you?' she said, catching on to his pointed sarcasm and narrowing her eyes.

'Power games?' He paused and thought about it. It *was* a test, of sorts. Would she sit there and tuck in, showing a devil-may-care attitude? Or would she refuse to touch it on principle?

The ball was in her court.

'It's just a sandwich, Tallulah,' he said, raising a derisive eyebrow and waiting for her move.

Their gazes locked and he found himself inappropriately turned on by engaging in this battle of wills with her. He was acutely aware of how intensely focused she was on him, as if she was trying to read his innermost thoughts. It was as if nothing but him existed in the world at that moment and it reminded him of how it had drawn him in the night before.

She played well, but she sure as hell was *not* going to win this.

Lula's heart beat so hard against her chest she thought it might escape at any second and run wildly around the room shouting, *She can't take the pressure; her head's about to explode!* She needed to keep calm and maintain some sort of composure here, but being this close to Tristan again was addling her already exhausted brain.

And she wanted to eat that bacon sandwich, *so* much, but she was afraid she'd look weak and lose the game and he'd hand her a P45 and wave her on her way without a second thought. On the other hand, perhaps she needed to *wo*man up here and show him she wasn't intimidated by his game-playing. To convince him she wasn't a liar or a manipulator like Jez.

Her reputation was on the line.

Resting her elbows on the arms of the chair and clasping her hands together in front of her, she considered her next move. The sensible thing to do was to brush aside her little white lie last night and bring the conversation back to her issue with Jez.

'Look, can we put aside what happened yesterday for now and focus on the reason for this meeting?' she said with as much composure as she could muster.

Tristan sat back in his chair and stared at her for a moment, one assessing eyebrow raised, before gesturing for her to continue.

She nodded her thanks and took a deep breath to try and even out her erratic breathing, fixing him with what she hoped was an emphatic-looking gaze.

Don't let me down now, brain.

'Jez has been subjecting me to sexual harassment for months. Recently he withdrew his promise to give me the Breakfast Show—which he currently hosts and should have moved me onto ages ago—because I wouldn't sleep with him.'

There was no need to mention the little 'slip-up' of already having slept with him—just because she'd given in once, it didn't mean she was obliged to again. She had a horrible feeling it might weaken her position if Tristan knew she'd already succumbed to Jez's advances, but most of all she was embarrassed to admit how weak-minded she'd been. She didn't want Tristan to think she was just some easy lay. It would taint the memory of the incredible night they'd had together.

She leant forwards in her seat. 'I deserve to be given that show on my own merit. I'm damn good at what I do, but when I made it perfectly clear I wasn't going to be blackmailed into sleeping with him he took me off my Drivetime Show too.' Her voice cracked at the end of the sentence and she cleared her throat and looked away from him, blinking away the hard pressure behind her eyes. This was no time for tears, but the mixture of stress, lack of sleep and confusion about how she felt about seeing Tristan again were playing havoc with her state of mind.

She longed for him to smile at her like he had last night. Just the quirk of a lip would do—anything, to break the icy atmosphere that had formed between them. But Tristan only nodded, his face devoid of expression.

'How long have you wanted the Breakfast Show?' he asked, his gaze averted as he picked up the tablet next to him and tapped something into it.

His sudden lack of attention made her go cold. She was losing him. 'Since I started working here. Hell, since I first started working on the radio. It's the best gig at the station. At any station.' Her voice sounded panicky and she took another calming breath before continuing. 'Jez promised me he'd stand aside and let me take over six months after I joined *Flash*, but he's hung on and hung on. He loves the status it gives him, but he can't run a show for toffee. He makes the station look amateurish.' Her voice had become louder and harsher the more she talked and she ended in a rush, her brow furrowed in a painfully tense scowl.

Damn her runaway mouth.

The way Tristan was silently studying her now was unnerving. There was no longer any sign of the playful, trusting man she'd been so intimate with only hours ago.

A tic jumped in her eye and her temple throbbed in time to its beat as she waited nervously for his response.

'I can see that you're very ambitious, Tallulah.'

The way he said it made it sound so seedy. The slow sinking feeling in her stomach told her he'd already made his decision and it wasn't to her benefit.

'The trouble is, Jeremy seems to be doing a good job here and he's made it perfectly clear he's not prepared to work with you any longer. He thinks you're disruptive and apparently you regularly turn up for your shift late. He suspects you've been drunk on at least one occasion whilst performing on-air.'

'What?' Her utter disgust that Jez would lie like that couldn't have been more clear, but Tristan seemed unmoved.

'I'm never late and I'm practically teetotal!' She flushed as she remembered the enormous glasses of wine he'd seen her drink the night before.

Of course he didn't believe her side of it; he'd met *Louise* last night.

Damn it. If she hadn't played that stupid pretend-to-be-someone-else game she wouldn't be in this mess right now.

'I know it looks bad right now, Tristan, but Jez is the liar here, not me.'

'Really, *Louise*.'

Her face flushed hot as he stared at her, his eyebrows raised in rebuke.

She looked away, trying to get her thoughts straight.

'You know what I think?' he said, leaning in and re-asserting eye contact with her. 'I think you knew who I was all along last night and decided you'd play me then leave me hanging in the hope I'd be so pleased to see you the next day I'd take your side over Jez's and you'd get the Breakfast Show you've always wanted.'

She gripped the table in anger. 'My God, who made *you* so paranoid?'

Clearly this was entirely the wrong thing to say because the expression on his face became fierce enough to melt steel.

'I've more reason to believe Jeremy's version of events right now.'

Her heart leapt in her chest and blood pounded in her head as she tried to get her next comeback straight through a fog of tiredness and tension. 'So, by your logic, just because I wanted to sleep with you, I must have made up the accusation about Jez pestering me to have sex with him again?'

There was a stunned silence as he looked at her, the corner of his mouth kicking up into a sardonic smile. 'So you were *already* sleeping with him.'

She frowned hard and shook her head in frustration, realising her slip-up. 'Yes. Once. But it was a mistake. Clearly a *huge* one. He caught me at a weak moment and I regret it.' She fisted her hands so hard her nails bit into her palms.

'Because he still wouldn't give you the Breakfast Show?'

'No!'

He held up a hand. 'To be honest, Tallulah, the whole thing sounds like sour grapes to me.' He tightened his arms across his broad chest. 'You wanted the Breakfast

Show and Jez wouldn't give it to you, even after you slept with him, so you decided to try every trick in the book to get rid of him so you'd get a clear shot at it.'

She could barely believe those words had just come out of his mouth. She'd thought he was a decent guy, but apparently she'd been very, *very* wrong about that.

'You know what *I* think, Tristan?' She could barely see straight, she was so offended. 'I think your father sent his errand boy to do his dirty work and clear up the mess his buddy's son made by brushing my concerns under the carpet. I never even had a chance to keep my job here because, unlike Jez, I'm not a friend of the family!'

Tristan's face was like stone, but she could see the anger flickering behind his eyes.

'You'd better pack up your desk, Tallulah, because I'm taking Jez's side on this one.' His voice was calm and flat, but very determined.

'What?' The word came out in a rush of air.

'You need me to spell it out for you?' He leaned in, bracing both hands against the table, his brow furrowed and his eyes cold. 'You're fired.'

CHAPTER FOUR

TRISTAN STARED OUT of the window after Tallulah walked out, feeling the anger slowly drain out of him. The look of disgust on her face when he'd lost his cool stayed with him like a burn mark on his vision and his stomach clenched with tension as he fought against a deep unease.

He'd never lost his temper with an employee before, but she'd overstepped the mark when she called him paranoid then accused him of being an *errand boy*.

As if.

He singlehandedly kept the family business afloat these days. If it had been left to his *missing in action* father or useless brother the whole portfolio would have collapsed around their ears by now. Increasingly, as the years went by, the old man had stopped thinking with his business head and put all his energy into partying and keeping his kaleidoscope of a love life rotating. In fact, Tristan would go so far as to say he'd turned into a world expert on the pursuit of women.

He remembered with a jolt of discomfort how his father had warned him about his relationship with Marcy at one point, suggesting he should ask her to marry him if he didn't want to lose her. He'd been so outraged with the patronising meddling he hadn't spoken to him for weeks. The old bugger had been right about her shaky commitment to him, though—just being with him hadn't been enough for her; she'd wanted his soul too.

And then Tallulah had swanned in today and chipped away at his already damaged dignity, making him react in an uncharacteristically rash manner.

Why were women hell-bent on reducing him to a heap of rubble?

There was a loud rap on the door and the Station Manager strolled in with a wide, confident smile on his pretty-boy face.

'Tristan. I'm Jeremy Whatley-Hume—but call me Jez.' He held out a hand, which Tristan took and shook, albeit diffidently. He didn't like the guy on sight.

'Thanks so much for coming in to sort out our little *problem*.' Jez gave the last word a flippant slant, as if it hadn't involved something as important as the altered trajectory of another person's career.

'We were meant to be meeting straight after your show finished, Jez,' Tristan said bluntly, allowing the remnants of his ire from the confrontation with Lu to spill into the tenor of his voice.

'Sorry about that,' Jez said, wafting a hand in Tristan's direction and flopping down into the chair Tallulah had just vacated, propping his feet up on the table and reclining back, not appearing sorry in the least. 'I had a last-minute meeting with an advertiser. Can't say no to the moneymen, Tristan,' he said, flashing what he clearly thought was a look of shrewd camaraderie, but actually made him seem more like a try-hard schoolboy.

Tristan didn't say anything; instead, he picked up his tablet and tapped some random nonsense into it, making Jez wait until he'd finished before they began the meeting.

Jez fidgeted beside him, obviously not used to being kept waiting for anything. 'So, she's gone then,' he blurted, unable to maintain the silence. 'Did she give you much trouble?' His tone was belligerently offhand, as if he hadn't doubted for a second that *she'd* be fired and not him.

Tristan's skin prickled with annoyance. There was something inherently unpleasant about the guy.

He didn't look up from his tablet. 'I've dealt with it. She's clearing her desk.'

Jez put his hands behind his head and stretched further back in his chair. If he got any more relaxed he'd be horizontal soon. 'Cheers for sorting it so quickly,' he said, yawning so wide Tristan could see his tonsils.

He was a handsome man, Tristan reflected; he could see why women might want to sleep with him, but surely they found his overconfident yapping a turn-off?

The thought of him and Tallulah together made his stomach roll unpleasantly.

'While I'm here, I'll take a look over the accounts,' he said to the side of Jez's head.

The guy seemed to stiffen and swivelled back to face Tristan, pinning him with an affronted expression. 'No need; they're all in order,' he drawled.

The attempted brush-off made Tristan wonder what he was hiding. 'I'll need to use your office while I go over them,' he said firmly, and was gratified to see a flash of annoyance on Jez's face.

Maybe it was childish, but he was enjoying seeing the guy shaken up.

'Okay, then,' Jez said, dropping his feet to the floor and standing up, apparently keen to be out of there now.

'I'll be out for most of the day—business to attend to—so it's all yours,' he muttered, not giving Tristan time to respond before he strode out, slamming the door closed behind him.

Tristan leaned back in his chair, a deep sense of foreboding invading his consciousness.

Something felt very wrong here.

'You have to sue the arse off them!'

Lula winced as Emily's voice bellowed down the phone at her. After stumbling home in a daze, she was now curled up on her overstuffed red velvet sofa wearing her tracksuit bottoms and a Take That T-shirt that she'd had since the early nineties. An empty packet of biscuits and a cold, half-full coffee mug sat on the table in front of her.

'It's not my style, Em; I couldn't take the stress of it. Anyway, I don't have money to spare to hire a lawyer and I'd probably do my professional reputation more harm than good by dragging this thing through a court.'

Emily snorted in disgust, but didn't push it. Her friend knew how much she hated confrontation.

'So what *are* you going to do?' Emily asked more gently.

'I've already been in touch with Scott Wendell. His long-standing job offer to present a show on his radio station in Melbourne is still open.'

'What? You'd really leave me and move all the way to Australia?'

Lula sighed, a thread of guilt tugging at her insides. 'Not everything revolves around you, Em.' She attempted to make a joke of it but it came out sounding more snippy than witty.

'I know, but I'd miss you like crazy.' Em's voice was

quieter now and, behind the exaggerated sulk, Lula detected a real twang of hurt.

'I don't *want* to go. I loved my job at *Flash*, but I have to be realistic. Even if by some miracle they gave me my show back, there's no way I could ever work for Jez again.' The thought of having to pander to him made her feel physically sick.

'Surely there's another station in London you could work for?'

Lula twisted her ponytail around her hand then let it slide through her fingers, finding comfort in the silky strands brushing against her skin. It was a move she'd done in times of stress since she was a little girl, especially when her parents had been having one of their screaming rows. 'I put my feelers out when things started getting sticky with Jez, but there's nothing out there at the minute. Not unless I want to take a big pay cut and work the graveyard shift, which would be a huge step backwards, career-wise.'

'Ugh! I can't believe they'd just fire you like that. The world's gone mad!'

Lula listened to her friend chunter on about the injustice of the situation with the pain in her chest and throat getting harsher by the second.

She hadn't even told Emily the whole story yet. She was afraid she'd totally lose it and burst into tears if she so much as mentioned Tristan's name. The fact he'd been so cold towards her had almost been worse than losing her job.

She'd really liked him last night.

So much so that she'd even entertained the notion that if she'd met him under different circumstances they could have made something of their connection. How unlucky *was* she to pull the one man she really needed to stay away from that night?

When she thought about it, it wasn't such a coincidence that they'd met, though. That pub was the closest one to the radio station, so of course they'd both naturally gravitated towards it. Her because it was her local from work and him because it made sense to stay close to where he was working the next day.

What bloody bad luck, though.

It had taken all her willpower to walk out of the station with her head held high and make it home without shedding the hot tears that burned at the back of her eyes. She knew that once she let the anger and panic get hold of her that would be it for the rest of the day—she'd be an emotional wreck. She'd wanted to get the practical stuff out of the way first so she could have a good old wallow without being disturbed.

'Look, I've got to go,' she told Emily, cutting her off mid-rant. She needed to get off the phone and finally let the growing hysteria free. 'I've got a whole tub of ice cream to scoff and many more hours of daytime TV to glom.' The effort to sound glib and in control almost made her choke. 'I'll speak to you tomorrow when I can formulate a coherent thought again, okay?'

There was a pause on the other end of the line. 'Okay, sweetie. You know where I am if you need me. I've got a couple of days off filming after tomorrow so I can come over in the blink of an eye and glom with you.'

'Thanks, Em. I really appreciate you being here for me. You're the only person I wanted to speak to, you know.'

'I know.' Emily did know. She'd been witness over the years to exactly how flaky Lula's parents were. From experience, they both knew neither of them would have returned a phone message from Lula for days. They were always too busy with their new families to get involved in the life of the daughter they'd had together. Neither of them wanted to take responsibility for her any more.

'I'll call you soon,' Lula said, keeping her voice as bouncy as she could manage.

'You do that.' Em's tone was kind now, which somehow made things worse.

Lula's throat tightened even more. 'Bye,' she squeaked and ended the call, finally letting her bravado slip and the long-held-back tears slide down her face.

Four hours after he'd first sat down at Jez's desk and begun to work his way through the files on his computer, Tristan knew why he'd been right to be worried about how the station was being run.

It seemed Jez had been playing fast and loose with the expenses account. Not only that, but there appeared to be a freelancer on the books—who was collecting an unusually high regular wage—that no one in the station had ever heard of. After doing some more digging, Tristan came to the conclusion that Jez had been paying himself a double wage by syphoning off the 'freelancer's' wage into his own account.

When he eventually caught up with Jez and interrogated him about it all, it was clear from the man's blustering anger that he realised he was busted. After playing the 'I've been working my arse off here for pathetic wages' card and bellowing the 'This station is going to die a terrible death without me' soliloquy, he finally gave Tristan enough air time to tell him he was fired.

'Your father's going to have something to say about

this when he gets back,' was Jez's parting shot before he stormed out, leaving Tristan's ears ringing with the sound of his histrionic ranting.

It was the second time that day that Tristan had been accused of playing second fiddle to his father and his blood thumped in his veins as he waited for his annoyance to abate. He couldn't believe his father had been so lax as to let someone like Jez have free rein with one of his businesses, even if he was the son of a friend. He'd be furious when he found out how much money Jez had been embezzling from him.

Although maybe it served the fool right for not paying more attention to his business affairs.

When Tristan finally felt calm enough, he called a meeting with the rest of the employees working at the station that day. They all filed into the conference room with pale faces, clearly expecting the firing spree to continue.

'Jez has been relieved as Station Manager,' he told them all once they'd taken their seats around the table.

There was a tense silence as they waited for him to continue.

He cleared his throat. He hadn't made much of a plan other than to get rid of Jez as soon as possible, but it was clear he was going to have to step in as a caretaker manager until he could find someone to take over full-time.

'I'm going to be here taking care of things until I can replace him so I'm going to need your cooperation,' he said, moving his gaze over the assembly.

The woman who had brought him the bacon sandwich that morning cleared her throat and raised a tentative hand.

He nodded for her to ask her question.

'Who's going to take over the Breakfast Show?'

'Er…' Tristan searched around wildly, his whole body growing hot with discomfort. In his rush to get rid of the guy, it had slipped his mind that Jez was a presenter here as well. 'Who would normally cover that show when he's away?'

The woman gave him a steady look. 'Tallulah Lazenby. She's the only one with enough experience to pick up such a tough show on short notice.'

Every single person around the table nodded their agreement.

'That's going to be a bit tricky,' Tristan said, smoothing an agitated hand over his hair. 'Because she doesn't work here any more.'

There was a stony silence, during which Tristan wondered what he'd done to deserve such an abysmal day.

The same woman spoke again, this time with a determined edge to her voice. 'Look, I don't know what Jez told you about Lula, but I can pretty much guarantee it was a pack of lies. She's the hardest working, most dedicated, most *professional* DJ we have at *Flash*. She should have been presenting the Breakfast Show ages ago, but Jez and his ginormous ego couldn't—or wouldn't—give it up.' Her face was flushed and she seemed to be trembling after her outburst, but she didn't break eye contact.

It was clear she meant every word and the fact the rest of the table was nodding along with her made him wonder whether he'd made a terrible mistake this morning firing Tallulah. Perhaps he'd let his humiliation at losing control of his actions get in the way of his usually dispassionate business thinking?

The sinking feeling in his gut made him think it almost certainly had. How could she have got under his skin in such a short amount of time and caused him to act so out of character?

He had no idea, but clearly she had.

And now it seemed he needed her in order to stop his father's pet project from crashing down around his ears. He had to find her and make things right.

He'd never been the type of man to run away from a mistake he'd made and he wasn't about to change that now.

Sighing, he ran a hand over his tired eyes.

Judging by the death stare Tallulah had given him on departing this morning, he suspected he was going to have his work cut out convincing her to come back.

Lula had finished all the ice cream, plus all the chocolate she had stashed in hiding places around the apartment and was just contemplating putting on a pair of sunglasses and her baseball cap to visit the local convenience store for more restorative refined sugar products when the buzzer went.

She sat stock-still on the sofa, hoping whoever it was would go away.

The buzzer went again, this time for longer, as if the person on the other side of her door knew she was holed up in there and was determined to speak to her.

Surely Emily wouldn't have walked out on her filming early to come over and watch TV when she'd made it clear she needed space right now.

No, Em knew her better than that.

So that meant it was someone else. Someone from work perhaps, come to commiserate with her?

Sighing, she levered herself off the sofa and went to check her appearance in the mirror.

She didn't look good. Her face was puffy after her

crying fit and her eyes looked dull and small. Whoever it was would get a real shock when she opened the door to them. Hopefully, her wild appearance would frighten them off so she could go back to her day of mooching and pity eating. She was only giving herself today to get it out of her system though, then she was bouncing back up and moving on. Just like she always did.

The buzzer went again, making her jump. Stumbling over to the door, she yanked it open and stared at the person waiting impatiently on the other side.

It took her a moment to fully comprehend who the tall, fit-looking man filling her doorway was and her stomach did a double somersault as his handsome face registered in her brain.

Tristan.

Inappropriate pleasure at seeing him again mixed with a blood-boiling indignation that he would have the gall to bother her at home after the way he'd treated her today. Pulling back her shoulders and tipping up her chin, she fixed him with a contemptuous stare.

His gaze dropped from her face to her feet and he tipped an eyebrow. 'You're not wearing your heels.'

She screwed up her face in confusion at the conversational curve ball. 'Of course not—I was relaxing on the sofa.' If you could call being curled up in a foetal position, clutching a soggy tissue relaxed, that was.

She instinctively lifted up onto her toes to try and give the impression of more height and power than she suspected she was projecting right at that moment.

The twitch of a grin at the corner of Tristan's mouth was the straw that broke her temper.

'What the hell are you *doing* here? Not come to accuse me of more dastardly deeds, have you? Because if you have you can bugger off and go stick your head right up—'

He cut off her ranting by taking a step forwards and holding up a placating palm.

'No. It seems I was a little too quick to judge the situation at *Flash*. Like you, I was a bit…er…tired this morning and it may have had an detrimental effect on my decision-making.'

Lula stared at him agog. 'I'm sorry—did I hear you right?' She shook her head and blinked hard, feigning the impression she must have misheard him. 'It sounded suspiciously like you were admitting you were wrong to fire me.'

'I think I may have made a mistake, yes, and I regret it.'

It looked as though it was causing him actual physical pain to admit he was in the wrong. Well, good.

She should drag this out, as revenge for his harsh treatment of her that morning.

'That constitutes an apology in Tristan World, does it?' she said coolly.

He frowned. 'Look, can I come in so we can discuss this?' he said, bracing one arm against the door jamb and dipping his head in a conciliatory manner.

Her body went up in flames as his wonderful scent hit her nostrils, bringing back memories of the enthralling feeling of his hard body beneath her only the night before.

Damn him for being such a low-down, dirty sex god.

She gave him a scrutinising look, playing for time while she attempted to get her head together. The thought of letting him into her sanctuary made her nervous. She was acutely aware of how bedraggled she looked—not to mention diminutive without her heels on—and she didn't want to give him the upper hand by feeling self-conscious about her appearance as well as the questionable state of her living room. There were sodden tissues and chocolate wrappers littering the coffee table and a line of underwear drying on the radiator behind the sofa. It didn't exactly shout, *You have no power over me. I'm moving onwards and upwards.*

'I'd rather do it here, if you don't mind. I don't want to be accused of luring you in here to take advantage of you again.'

He let out a snort, but quickly reined in his mirth.

'Okay, Tallulah, fair enough.'

'So what prompted this *revelation*?' she asked, folding her arms in front of her ancient, faded T-shirt, hoping he hadn't noticed the adolescent boy band motif on the front.

Tristan frowned and rubbed a hand over his jaw, his fingers making a faint rasping sound against the beginnings of his stubble. His gaze flicked around her hallway before snapping back to her. He suddenly looked very tired and for a second she almost felt sorry for him. Almost.

He huffed out a breath. 'It seems Jez has been misappropriating money from the station and, after talking with some of the other staff, it appears you were right about him taking certain other liberties with his position as well.'

Lula stared at him, dumbfounded. 'Really? God. So you fired him?' she asked hopefully. It would serve the idiot right if he'd been booted too.

'Yes. He's gone and I'm stepping in to manage the station until I can find a suitable replacement.' He bit down on his lip as if he was keying himself up to add something else.

Lula's gaze was drawn to his mouth as he uttered the next words.

'We need you back at *Flash*. Now Jez has gone I can offer you the Breakfast Show slot. Apparently you're the best and most experienced presenter at the station and the general consensus is that it should go to you.'

Her mouth tingled, like sherbet fizzing on her tongue, as she thought about kissing that full mouth of his with joy at the news. Now the ball was in her court she could probably do whatever she wanted to him and he'd have to put up with it if he wanted her back. And he evidently did, considering he'd come all the way over here after hours with his tail between his legs to talk to her.

Of course he needed someone with her experience to take over the Breakfast Show. It would be virtually impossible to find someone else with the skills needed to step in at such short notice and do a good job.

He needed *her*.

She had a flash of memory about how empowering it had felt to call the shots with him last night and wondered whether she could bring herself to do it again. To get her own back on him for his unfair treatment of her today.

The memory of Tristan's cold expression when he'd fired her sprang into her mind again and the decision was made. She'd be lax if she didn't make him work at least a little bit hard for her forgiveness. She was sick of putting up with men pushing her around and taking her good nature for granted.

'So what are you offering me?' she asked, tipping up her chin.

He frowned, appearing confused. 'I'm offering you your job back and the opportunity to take over the Breakfast Show, which I know you've been interested in for quite some time.'

'Yes, I got that. I mean what sort of wage hike are you offering? How far are you going to extend my contract on the show to make sure I'm allowed a good run at it? Perks, that kind of thing.'

He stared at her, the surprise clear in his eyes. Apparently he thought he could waltz over here, toss her the offer of the Breakfast Show and she'd fall on her knees in gratitude.

Well, you can think again, Mister.

Even though she wanted that show with a passion, she needed to go back to the station feeling as though she had some power in her new position and wouldn't just be ousted by a new Station Manager the moment Tristan slunk off back to Edinburgh.

He closed his eyes and laughed to himself, shaking his head as if he couldn't believe what he'd got himself into here. Of course, he'd only meant to come over for the day to dish out his father's orders and he'd somehow found himself with a mutiny on his hands.

That would teach him to get involved in other people's affairs.

'Okay,' he said, running a hand over his, by now, rather rumpled hair. 'You can have a ten per cent wage increase to reflect your importance to the station and we'll give you a year-long contract to show our commitment to you.'

She raised her eyebrows, but didn't say anything.

Tristan cleared his throat and narrowed his eyes. 'Okay, playing hardball, huh? A two-year contract and fifteen per cent wage hike.'

'I'd expect nothing less than a three-year contract and twenty per cent,' she said levelly, digging her nails into her palms under her crossed arms to force herself to stand tough.

There was a long pause while Tristan digested her demands, his pragmatic gaze raking her face.

Finally, he nodded, drawing himself up to his full height as he pushed himself away from the doorframe and stood back.

A bubble of glee rose from deep inside her, making her skin tingle all over. She'd bloody well *done* it. She'd beaten him into submission.

Despite the urge to blurt out her acceptance of his terms and get straight down to the time-consuming business of planning the show for the morning, she made herself take a breath and a mental step away. After all, she'd had a tough day and shouldn't jump into anything without giving it some proper consideration first.

It occurred to her too that he hadn't apologised for accusing her of sleeping with him to sway his decisions.

She needed to hold her nerve for a bit longer to totally pay him back and restore her pride.

He was looking at her confidently, waiting for her agreement, his expression more relaxed now he seemed to think he'd sorted out the mess he'd made.

Flipping him as assertive a smile as she could muster, she put her hand on the door and straightened her posture, hoping he wouldn't notice how much she was trembling.

'Thanks for coming over. I have another job offer on the table, so I'll think about yours and let you know my decision soon.'

He looked at her as if she'd just spoken complete gibberish. 'But I need you at work tomorrow.'

She smiled sweetly. 'Sorry, I have plans tomorrow. But I'll get back to you in the next day or two.'

He opened and closed his mouth, apparently lost for words.

'Bye, Tristan.' She swung the door shut in his face, hearing it close with a satisfying *click*.

CHAPTER FIVE

TRISTAN HAD NEVER been so stressed in his life.

It had taken him the rest of the evening to find someone willing to step in to present the Breakfast Show on such short notice. Darla, the woman who had taken over Tallulah's old Drivetime Show, point-blank refused to help him out because of the way he'd treated Jez 'so appallingly' and the rest of the presenters seemed unwilling to help because he'd fired Tallulah.

Added to that, he'd spent the night tossing and turning in his hotel bed as flashes of her face kept springing into his head. She knew *exactly* the trouble she was causing him—he'd seen the mischief in her eyes as she'd swung the door shut in his face.

Admittedly, he'd been floored when she'd refused to take his more than generous offer right away, but after chewing on it for a while he wondered whether he'd actually deserved the rejection. In his rush to get past his frustration about the night he'd spent with her, he'd not done his job properly and let his emotions get in the way of common sense.

He should have tried to smooth things over with her first.

Clearly this problem wasn't going to be resolved with cold hard cash like most things he came across in his life either. Judging by the fact she lived in a large, swanky apartment in central London perhaps money wasn't her driving force. Maybe she had wealthy parents or a large inheritance behind her? Her wage from the radio station certainly wouldn't have covered a mortgage, or even the rent, on a place like that.

Whatever it was that drove her, she'd certainly got his attention.

Unsurprisingly, the Breakfast Show was a total chaos of missed cues and fumbled links and the poor guy who he'd pulled from the sleepy graveyard shift to take over let Tristan know in no uncertain terms that he wasn't prepared to do it again the following day.

There had been a fair number of complaints from the listeners too.

If Tristan weren't careful, the advertisers—who kept the station running with their regular imbursements—would start making a fuss and then they'd be in real trouble.

Unfortunately, his father wasn't contactable for another month as he and his new yoga-obsessed wife had decided to shroud themselves in solitude in the middle of Asia to 'become one with the earth' so it was totally down to Tristan to handle things here.

He'd already arranged for Andrew, his second-in-command at the company he ran from Edinburgh, to carry on caretaking in his place whilst he was down here in London so he could concentrate fully on getting the station back up and running with a new manager.

Right now, his main priority was to get Tallulah to agree to return tomorrow. He suspected he'd need to be creative about how he went about it too, because, without a doubt, she was holding off on giving him an answer to pay him back for firing her in the first place.

And perhaps for his less than objective suggestion that she'd only slept with him to gain a competitive edge. Hot embarrassment trickled through him as he remembered the accusations he'd made in the heat of the moment.

It hadn't been his finest hour.

He had to have imagined all her slightly odd behaviour when they first met, retrofitting it afterwards into his conviction that she'd been playing him for a fool, when maybe it had been something else? But what?

Not that he should be worrying about that at the moment. He needed to focus on the job in hand.

He sat for a few minutes staring into space as he considered the best way to get her attention.

Lightning finally struck.

He smiled, an unexpected feeling of excitement rising from deep within his chest. She liked playing games? Well, okay then, he was going to present her with the best brain-teaser of her life.

Tallulah slept in late and woke to find bright sunlight streaming in through the chinks in her curtains.

After all the tension of the previous day, it was absolute bliss to lie there for a while and not have to spring out of bed to get ready for her shift at work.

Not that she could hold off from giving Tristan an answer for long. She knew she couldn't push him too hard, or he'd soon find someone else to step in and snap up her contract. The benefits of having experience on the show and a good track record at the station would only give her the edge over a newcomer for so long.

Still, it had been satisfying to see the comical stunned expression on his face when she'd shut the door on him. It had more than made up for the cold look of disapproval she'd last experienced on that handsome face of his.

Unbidden memories from their night together swam through her head as she thought about him, leaving a warm afterglow in the most intimate of places. She wriggled around in frustration, clamping her thighs together to quell the sensation. The very last thing she should be doing was lusting after Tristan again. Look what kind of mess she'd got herself into when she'd last given in to that impulse.

No. Sadly, that had to have been the one and only time there was any intimacy between them. The man was a shark.

Her reflections were interrupted by the sound of the buzzer.

Hauling herself out of bed and wrapping up in her large towelling robe, she raced to the door, half wondering in a nervy excited way whether it would be Tristan again. The Breakfast Show couldn't have been a roaring success with no one at the station with experience in hosting it to take over at such short notice. Perhaps he'd come to camp out on her doorstep until she agreed to come back? Her heart did a loop-the-loop as she pictured stepping over Tristan's gorgeous prostrate body on her way out for milk.

Hmm, she quite liked the idea of that.

It was a flower delivery. The bouquet was so large she could hardly see the delivery person behind it. After accepting it with an excited squeak, she carried it into the living room and set it on the coffee table, brushing aside the debris from the day before to make room for it. As she looked at it more carefully, she realised there were jigsaw pieces with words written on them spiked on sticks and dotted in amongst the flowers.

After rummaging through the whole bouquet and

finding sixteen different pieces, she made room on the table so she could fit them together and make up the handwritten note. Once she'd completed it she stared in amusement at the words spelled out in front of her:

Since you've been gone, things around here have fallen to pieces...

There wasn't a name anywhere on the note. Even so, she had a strong suspicion she knew who it was from. A burst of laughter bubbled up from inside her and broke free. Was this Tristan's way of trying to persuade her to agree to take back the job? If so, it was a pretty good shot.

Leaning down, she sniffed the beautiful fragrant bouquet, delighting in the heady mixture of scents as they wound through her nostrils. No one had ever bought her flowers as grand as this before and they certainly hadn't gone to the trouble of leaving her a message to puzzle out.

Standing up, she shook herself. She really shouldn't let a few stems and a jigsaw turn her head so easily. It was important to remember that he needed something from her and there wasn't any kind of romance in the gesture. It was purely mercenary on his part.

She took herself off for a shower, mulling it all over, and just as she got out there was the loud rasp of the buzzer again.

Hurrying to the door in just a towel—praying it really *wasn't* Tristan this time—she pulled it open to reveal a tall, lanky youth with a brown cardboard box in his hands.

'I have a delivery for Tallulah Lazenby,' he said, desperately trying to keep his gaze averted from her dripping wet, skimpily towelled body and looking somewhere off to the left of her head, his eyes wide and the skin on his neck flushed a deep red.

'Thanks,' Lula said, taking the box gently from him. 'Where has it come from?'

'I work at The Magic Store on Oxford Street. A customer gave me fifty quid to come over and deliver this to you in my break.' He still couldn't meet her eyes and she decided to be kind and put him out of his misery. 'Thanks very much.' She gave him a nod to release him and he backed away quickly and ran off down the hallway leading out of her apartment block.

She opened up the box right there by the door. It looked as if there was a glass ball inside. Lifting it out carefully, she examined it. It sat on a wooden base and the whole thing was heavy and solid, the glass thick.

It took her a few seconds to realise what she was holding. It was a fortune-teller's crystal ball.

Shaking her head, she laughed to herself.

Nice.

He'd remembered her flip remark about how being able to see into the future would be a useful skill. It really *would* have been the night they'd met. None of this mess with Tristan would have happened if they'd both known what was about to unfold.

Carrying it into the living room, she put the ball on the sideboard and turned her attention back to the box. There was an envelope taped to the top of it, which she tore open, shifting the cardboard box under one arm so she could hold up the note and read it.

Once I realised, I wanted to let you know...

Once he realised what? That he'd been an arrogant arse for not even listening to her side of the story before jumping to conclusions?

That he liked her a lot more than he was letting on and wanted to see her again in a non-work capacity?

Even though the thought of that gave her a warm flutter in her belly, she knew she needed to quash it quickly. There couldn't be any more sexy times with him—she wasn't going to sleep with someone she worked for ever again.

No.

Not going to happen.

Tossing the card onto the table, she went to get dressed and dry her hair.

She was in the kitchen making herself a cup of tea when the buzzer went for the third time.

Fishing the tea bag out of the cup so as not to stew her drink, she went to answer the door again.

Since the last note had arrived she'd turned the question of what he would write next over and over in her mind, spending rather more time than she should have thinking about him.

The guy knew exactly what he was doing—she had to give him credit for that.

A tall, raven-haired lady with a bright red-lipsticked smile waited patiently on the other side of her door. Lula recognised her from the café round the corner—the place that did the most amazing breakfasts.

The smell of the bacon sandwich the woman was now proffering hit her nostrils. Lula's stomach rumbled and her mouth filled with saliva in anticipation of the intensely sweet, salty taste of the bacon and the glorious soft bloomer roll. She took the sandwich and thanked the still beaming lady, who waved away her offer of money. 'It's already been taken care of,' she said, giving Lula one last knowing grin.

She only noticed the writing on the greaseproof

wrapper—which appeared to be in different handwriting to the rest of the notes—after she'd shut the door. He must have got the lady from the café to write it.

It read:

Right or wrong—wrong as it turns out—I thought I was making things right...

Huh.

Well, at least he'd fully admitted he was wrong to fire her, even if he was still trying to defend his actions.

She stared at the sandwich in her hand, which looked and smelled all delicious and tempting.

Well, there was no sense in wasting food. She peeled back the wrapper and sank her teeth into the soft floury roll.

Heavenly.

It was just after lunchtime when the next delivery arrived. Lula rushed to the door, trying not to get too excited, aware of the manic beat of her heart and how foolish it was to allow herself to respond like this.

This time a courier held out something the size and shape of a shoebox to her.

She took it inside and opened it up.

It was a pair of black mule-style slippers with six-inch heels and a fluff of feathers framing the open toe.

She'd never have to answer the door feeling short again.

There was a strange tingling feeling behind her eyes as she opened the note attached to the shoebox.

Respect to you for standing your ground...

Something squeezed hard in her chest. Brushing the feeling off, she stooped and slid the slippers onto her feet. They were totally over the top for wearing indoors and she'd never owned anything so ridiculous in her life—but she loved them.

Striding into her bedroom, she stood in front of the long cheval mirror and stared at her reflection. She couldn't help but laugh, the impulse surging up in great bursts of joy from deep inside her.

It had been a long time since she'd felt this buzzed.

Staring out of the window, she toyed with the idea of going out. The sun was pouring down onto an unseasonably bright and balmy London, but she couldn't quite be bothered.

It had absolutely nothing to do with wanting to see what Tristan would send next or what might be written in the note that came with it.

Nothing at all.

Just as the discomfiting heat of her self-denial began to warm her face, there was another loud jolt on the buzzer.

A brand-new pair of top-of-the-range headphones was waiting for her this time. She signed the courier's electronic pad and took them eagerly into the house, pulling them out of the box to study them properly. She'd been meaning to get herself a pair of these for a while. They had amazing sound quality and were incredibly comfortable, which was imperative when you had to wear them for hours at a time.

He'd really thought about all his gifts, targeting them directly at her needs and whims.

Clever. Very clever.

She pulled off the note taped to the box and read it with her heart in her mouth.

You are appreciated. We need you here. Please come back.

PS If you line the cards up, the first vertical row will tell you how I'm feeling right about now.
PPS I'll be picking you up for dinner at eight p.m. and we'll get into those 'perks' that we never got around to discussing yesterday.
Wear what you like. I suspect you look good in everything you own.
Tristan

Exhilaration, driven by pure unadulterated excitement, shot straight through her. What did he mean by 'perks'? Was he referring to business-type bonuses or an altogether more saucy sort of incentive?

Her heart banged in her chest and she had to sit down as the sudden excess of adrenaline made her woozy.

She read the note still clutched in her trembling fingers again: *...line the cards up, the first vertical row will tell you how I'm feeling...*

Gathering all the notes together, she placed them one above the other in the order they'd been sent and scanned down the first letter of each word.

SORRY

It felt as though something tight and hard had finally broken inside her, coating her insides with a delicious warmth.

Okay, so he was capable of apologising properly and he certainly didn't do things by halves, but the man was so presumptuous telling her to be ready to go out at eight o'clock when he had no idea whether she was busy tonight or even prepared to give him her answer yet.

She couldn't stop a wide grin from breaking across her face.

She really liked that about him. She liked it a lot.

Quite possibly more than she should.

* * *

Tristan smoothed down his hair one more time before pressing the buzzer to Tallulah's apartment.

He hoped the deliveries he'd sent over had softened her up a little—at least enough to give him an opportunity to talk her round.

After all his years of heading up a business, he couldn't believe he'd propelled the radio station into such turmoil after he'd only been responsible for it for one day. He'd never made such an ill thought-out, emotionally driven mistake in his life and it was all down to the woman who lurked behind this door.

He seemed to have found his nemesis.

He'd been thinking about her all day, wondering what her reactions had been to each present and feeling a strange disappointment that he hadn't been there to witness her delight—or disdain—as each one arrived.

He hadn't wanted to admit it to himself earlier, but he was actually looking forward to taking her out to dinner this evening and having the opportunity to get to know her a little better.

Not that he was expecting any kind of serious relationship to develop here—he wasn't ready for that so soon after the fallout of the last one—but he wouldn't say no to another night in the sack with her.

Would she even entertain the notion?

He had absolutely no clue.

The woman was a total conundrum, so much so, he had no idea what to expect when Lu opened the door to him this time—assuming that she *did* of course. Maybe she'd have deliberately gone out to make a point.

At least the things he'd sent over seemed to have been taken in and hadn't been left in a rejected heap by her front door.

He waited, nerves thrumming, for a few more seconds before reaching for the buzzer again. He didn't want to seem too eager. Based on his previous experience with her, he needed to keep his cool if he was in with a chance of resolving this quickly and successfully.

Just as he gave in to his impatience and moved to push the buzzer again the door swung open to reveal Tallulah in all her glory.

And she really did look glorious. She was wearing a knee-length black dress that hugged her voluptuous curves. The neckline was low, but not too revealing, giving a tantalising glimpse of those magnificent breasts and her hair was swept back into some sort of elegant knot at the back of her head. She looked businesslike but classy. And very sexy.

'You look lovely,' he said, experiencing a swell of satisfaction as he clocked her answering smile.

'You weren't expecting to find me dressed for dinner?' She looked back at him from under her eyelashes with mischief in her expression.

He battled to ignore an extra hard pulse of sexual heat as he recognised it as the same look she'd given him the other night in his hotel room.

'To be honest, you're a bit of an unknown quantity at the moment,' he said on a grin.

She chuckled. 'Actually, I did consider going out in my band T-shirt, sweats and heeled slippers—which I love by the way—but I thought it might seem rather petty.'

He nodded; pleased she'd acknowledged the slippers and seemed to have appreciated the gesture. He'd worried that that particular present could have gone down very badly, considering how touchy she seemed to be about her height. Luckily humour appeared to have won out. 'So you went for pretty over petty.'

Colour flushed across her cheeks at his blatant flattery.

'You're full of compliments today, aren't you?' she purred, the tone of her voice implying she knew his game and wasn't falling for it that easily.

'Just trying to claw back some goodwill,' he said, leaning in closer to her.

She took a small step back and narrowed her eyes; giving him such a taunting look he felt the power of it deep in his chest. Desire rushed more heat down his spine, but he swept away his urge to push her up against the wall and kiss that look right off her face.

He needed to stay focused and remember they had business to take care of first.

Clenching his hands into fists for strength against the tempting urges, he gestured back out into the hallway of the apartments. 'So, are you ready?'

'Yes,' she said, turning to grab her bag and coat from a hook on the wall.

'Then let's go.'

Tristan had called in a favour from a friend and snagged a table at his new restaurant, which was currently the hippest—and most eye-wateringly expensive—joint in town, wanting to ram home to Tallulah that he wasn't messing about here.

After the taxi dropped them off outside, he guided her in through the large dark-tinted glass doors and gave his name to the maître d'.

They were ushered through the dining room, which appeared to be styled like some kind of 1970s diner—all dark wooden panels, squared off chrome fixtures and boxy orange leather booths—to an octagonal, glass-topped table at the back.

Their waiter brought over complimentary glasses of Appletini and a small bowl of spiced nuts while they perused the menu.

Neither of them said anything to the other until they'd given their food and drink orders, but the tension hummed between them like a stripped livewire.

Lula was the first to break the silence as she watched their waiter walk away.

'So.' She crossed her arms in front of her, which automatically drew his eyes to her impressive chest.

He flicked his gaze back up quickly, not wanting to be caught ogling her. Damn, if this wasn't doing his head in. It wouldn't have been so bad if he didn't already know how amazing she felt pressed against him and how sweet she'd tasted. How moreish.

Shifting in his seat, he tried not to give away how turned on he was just from sitting opposite her with those incredible memories dancing through his head. 'So. Thank you for coming back to *Flash*.'

She smiled down at the table. 'I haven't agreed to it yet.'

'Ah, but you will.'

Her gaze snagged with his. 'You're very sure of yourself.'

He shrugged. 'We both know *Flash* has the potential to be an outstanding radio station—which means accolades and upward career moves for anyone working there—and that you're the best DJ there by a mile. Everyone I've spoken to says so.'

She was looking at him with a concentrated frown on her face now, which she forced into a sad little smile when he raised a questioning eyebrow at her.

'It's really nice to hear that,' she said. 'No one's ever told me that before. Jez wasn't particularly good at boosting staff morale.'

'So I've heard.'

'I guess I should thank you for taking my concerns seriously. In the end.'

He leant forwards, splaying his hands onto the table in front of him in a gesture of total openness. 'Look, I apologise for that. I wasn't as focussed as I should have been during that session. Meeting you and doing what we did,' he shifted in his seat as his body responded to the memories again, 'wasn't the norm for me. I've just come out of a four-year relationship and wasn't looking for that to happen. It caught me by surprise, and I'm not good with surprises.'

He took a sip of his drink to cover his discomfort. It was harder than he'd anticipated, talking about how he'd reacted to what had happened. It was bringing back the rumblings of unease he'd been supressing since Marcy had left him.

He shook it off and focussed his attention back on her.

She was giving him a speculating look. Was she wondering about how they moved forwards from here too?

'I hope it won't effect our working relationship because once you come back,' he gave her a meaningful look, 'you're going to have to put up with having me as your boss until I can find a new Station Manager to take over.'

She stared at him for a moment, her eyes wide, then nodded slowly. 'I guess I should thank you for all the gifts and notes you sent today. I'm very impressed that you remembered all that about me.' She tucked an errant strand of hair behind her ear and he noticed her fingers were shaking.

'I bet no woman has ever resisted your wooing,' she continued, smiling now. 'If the way you handle your relationships is anything like the way you handle business affairs, they wouldn't stand a chance. I bet they're putty in your hands!'

From the colour of her cheeks it was clear she thought she'd said too much and he experienced an unnerving urge to help her out of her babble loop.

'To be honest, I've never sent a woman flowers before.' He frowned. 'Not that I should be admitting to that.'

'Really?' she raised her eyebrows. 'Maybe that's why your last relationship broke up.' She followed her comment with a smile, which quickly dropped off her face when she saw he wasn't smiling back.

It had suddenly struck him, like a lead bar to the stomach, that he'd never sent anything of a personal nature to Marcy, or any of his other girlfriends, come to think of it. He'd bought them things, sure, but the gifts had never been targeted to them as individuals. They'd been cold, hard objects—symbols of his wealth and status.

He gave himself an internal shake. Time to move the conversation away from him and back onto her.

'What led you to become a DJ?' he asked, leaning back in his chair and attempting to relax his tense shoulders.

'I like the way it allows me to be in control of the conversation.' She flashed him a self-conscious grin, which he returned this time.

There was a pause in which she straightened her cutlery on the table.

'I spent a lot of time in my own head when I was young and there's something really freeing about being given a microphone to speak into without having to see people's reactions to what you're saying. Also, I like that people are interested in my opinions and that I can spark interesting conversations with the power of my voice.'

Her cheeks were pink again and he wondered which bit of her answer had made her uncomfortable.

'Why did you spend so much time in your own head?'

Her gaze flicked to meet his, the expression in her eyes wary.

Yup. That bit.

She sighed. 'My parents were really young when they had me and hadn't been together very long—they met at University. Obviously, I wasn't planned. They were both ambitious and wanted to build their careers and didn't exactly have a harmonious relationship. They're both really fiery tempered and after one of their arguments they often wouldn't speak to each other for weeks.'

She gave a little shiver. 'There's a very particular type of silence between two people who are angry with each other and it made for a really tense atmosphere in the house. I was their only medium of communication—I had to pass messages between them—and I used to get caught in the crossfire of resentment.' She grimaced and put the tips of two fingers against her temple, pretending to pull a trigger. 'Shooting the messenger.'

'Sounds hellish.'

'Yeah, well, it wasn't a lot of fun. I'm not a big fan of confrontation so I spent a lot of time hiding out in my room.'

'You're an only child?'

'I was then. I have two half-sisters on my mum's side and a stepbrother on my dad's now.'

He nodded, starting to understand where she was coming from.

'They were very good at providing all the material stuff I needed though, can't fault them for that,' she said, with a forced brightness in her voice. 'My dad paid to put me through University and bought me my apartment to live in. He's very good at buying his way out of a problem.' She pinched her eyebrows together in derision.

Tristan felt another thump of disquiet as he thought about how he'd been guilty of the same behaviour whenever he'd upset Marcy by point blank refusing to discuss getting married.

'What did they argue about?' he asked, not wanting to dwell on the troubling insight.

'Ugh! Everything—although mainly about whether they were going to get married.'

His stomach sank further as he realised he'd walked out of the frying pan and straight into the conversational fire.

'My mum really wanted to, but my dad was dead against it,' Lula continued, totally oblivious to how much this topic was making him squirm. 'I think my mum felt he didn't love her enough to make the commitment and it eroded their relationship so much she went off and had an affair, which split them up. She's married to the guy she cheated on my dad with now and couldn't be happier.'

Tristan snorted, appalled that she clearly believed matrimony was some sort of magic fix. 'Really? My father's been married five times and it's never made him happy.'

'Wow, that's—er—' She was clearly lost for words.

'Obscene? Yeah. My mum died when I was twelve and he got married again six months after we buried her.'

'How did that make you feel?'

He shrugged. 'At the time I was really angry because it was as if he was disrespecting my mum's memory by moving on so fast—as if she hadn't even existed, but I came to realise he just couldn't bear to be alone.'

He cocked a disparaging eyebrow. 'I wouldn't have minded so much, but I'd just started to get to like my new stepmother when he dumped her and moved on to the next one. Then the next one, then the next.'

He snorted and ran a hand over his hair. 'I stopped letting myself get close to any of his wives or girlfriends pretty quickly after that. As far as I've seen, marriage is nothing but an expensive court case waiting to happen.'

He looked at her to find she was staring at him in dismay.

He flipped her a grin. 'Hey, just ignore me, it's a subject that gets me fired up. That's all.'

She frowned as if she'd found what he said sad.

Luckily, their food arrived then and they tucked in, giving him a few moments to pull himself together.

What the hell was he doing talking to her about this stuff? They barely knew each other and here he was spilling his guts. He needed to slap a lid on that quickly—but she was just so easy to talk to with her open expression and kind eyes.

'So, what are these *perks* you mentioned in your note?' she murmured after another minute of silence, not looking at him while she worked her knife carefully through her sirloin steak.

He rested his cutlery on the plate while he addressed

her question, glad to get back to a subject he felt comfortable with. 'Well, Jez had a company mobile phone and a taxi allowance for getting to any functions he attended as the lead presenter at the station…'

He ran through a couple of other entitlements, which to him made the whole deal sound like something someone would be crazy to turn down. When he'd finished, she nodded and gave a small controlled smile. Could she really have been expecting more? 'That's a good package, Tallulah.'

Her gaze met his and something like disappointment flashed across her face.

'It's a very good package,' she said, sounding as though she really believed it. So why the long face?

He decided to wait until they'd finished eating before pressing on with more business talk, asking her instead about what she liked about living in London and how she spent her downtime.

It turned out they liked to do the same kinds of things: taking long walks on a Sunday morning, eating Indian food, checking out photography exhibitions. The more they talked, the more he found himself relaxing into her company again. She was a superb dinner companion, receptive and responsive in turn—the things that had drawn him to her the other night—and he had to remind himself a couple of times that he wasn't here on a date with her.

Unless they both decided to take things further again later. His body hardened at the thought.

'So, are you happy with the terms of my offer?' he asked, when they'd both cleared their plates and waved away the suggestion of dessert. A coil of tension tugged at his insides as he waited for her answer. Surely he'd done enough to clinch her return?

'Yes,' she said finally, leaning back in her chair looking at him with her bright, steady gaze, the corner of her mouth twitching up into a smile.

'Yes?' he repeated, hoping against hope that she was agreeing to come back to *Flash* but needing to hear those exact words come out of her mouth before he believed it.

'I'm accepting your offer of reemployment and promotion to Breakfast Presenter.'

He was so relieved he could have kissed her. In fact he had to grip the edge of the table to stop himself from leaping out of his seat and pulling her out of her chair into his arms.

She must have sensed this impulse because she fixed him with a hard stare. 'You understand that nothing else can happen between us now though, right? I can't work for you if everyone at the station thinks we're sleeping together. I'll lose all credibility with my co-workers and I'm not prepared to let that happen. It's really important to me that they respect and trust me so we can function as a team on equal terms. Getting into bed with the boss isn't something that would go down well. Trust me, I know.'

All the joy had slowly drained out of him as she'd talked, but he managed to nod confidently, clinging on to his professionalism by a thread. 'Of course, I didn't come here expecting anything more from you. Just that you'd take your job back.' He swept a conciliatory hand in her direction, ignoring his self-disgust at voicing such a convincing sounding lie. 'There wouldn't be any point in us pursuing anything other than a business relationship anyway. As soon as I've found a replacement for Jez I'll be back off to Edinburgh. Back to my life there.'

He could have sworn he saw another flash of disappointment in her face, before she formed a smile and tipped her head in agreement.

She *must* still feel the same pull of desire that he did. He didn't believe she could shake him off so easily after what they'd shared. The need to know he was right prodded at the edges of his control.

The next few weeks were going to be a trying time if he had to keep his hands off her, but it didn't mean he had to totally ignore the irrefutable connection between them.

There was still some fun to be had here.

CHAPTER SIX

OVER THE NEXT couple of days they managed to maintain a friendly, but businesslike atmosphere between them, although Lula made sure to leave the room as quickly as was polite so she didn't have to deal with the weird, tight ache in her chest that appeared whenever he did.

Tristan's revelations about his aversion to marriage and recent split from a long-term partner had sealed her decision not to get further involved with him.

Clearly he wanted different things in life to her and no way was she going to be his rebound woman—she'd been through the humiliation of that before and wasn't prepared to do it again. They always seemed to go back to their exes as soon as she settled into the hope things might work between them.

And he was her boss, which made up the triumvirate of a no-go.

She had a duty to protect herself from any relationship that was destined to bring her more pain and loneliness. She'd had enough of that to last her a lifetime.

It didn't stop her from wanting him though, which was a bit of a problem when she had to see him every day.

She'd quickly got into the routine of her new show, and even though it left her both mentally and physically drained, she'd never been happier with that part of her life.

The whole atmosphere at *Flash* had changed since Tristan had stepped into the breach. Everyone seemed less guarded and more relaxed than when Jez was in charge—which wasn't surprising as the man had had a unique gift for getting people's backs up.

She was desperate that no one at the station should find out what had happened between her and Tristan though and terrified she would give herself away when she was near him.

It had been bad enough when the whispers had gone around about her succumbing to Jez's 'charms'. Any time someone had so much as mentioned her and Jez's name in the same sentence she'd wanted to bury her head in the ground in shame. It had caused a really uncomfortable atmosphere for a while and no one had wanted to take her into their confidence in case word got back to Jez about their grievances.

No way would she be able to hold her head high if everyone knew she'd had sex with Tristan too.

Sleeping with one of her bosses could be seen as careless. Sleeping with two was just plain stupid.

She was taking her customary time out after the show on Friday morning when Tristan came into one of the offices where she liked to hide out. Her heartbeat picked up as she tried not to notice how ridiculously sexy he looked today with his shirt open at the neck and his sleeves rolled up to his elbows, displaying his strong, tanned forearms. His transformation into casual cool messed with her head. It was so much easier to compartmentalise him when he was all buttoned up in his restricting suit somehow.

'Hey,' he said, giving her a nod, 'I wondered where you got to after you finished your shows.'

She scrambled to sit up on the sofa and straightened her T-shirt, which had ridden up, exposing her midriff. 'I like to have a bit of quiet time after I come off-air—to reflect, you know? Before I start planning for the next show.'

He'd dropped his gaze down her body when she'd pulled on her clothing and when he looked her in the eye again his pupils were large and dark.

Awareness tickled down her spine.

Giving her a slow knowing smile he walked over to the sofa and sat down next to her, so close she could smell the heady masculine scent of him. Exotic spice with the dark undertone of alpha male.

Leaning an elbow against the back of the sofa, he propped his head in his hand and studied her, his eyes roaming her face. 'I wasn't criticising you, just making an observation.'

Her heart was thumping so hard in her chest she suspected her body must be visibly pulsing with it. Was he deliberately sitting this close to get a reaction out of her? She had a strong suspicion he was. Clearly he wasn't taking their pact as seriously as she was.

She was going to have to pay him back for that.

Crossing her arms, she gave him an *I know your game* smile. 'Was there something you needed from me?'

Straightening his posture, he arranged his face into a more businesslike expression. 'Yes. I've put out a couple of adverts for a new Station Manager and I'm starting to get some replies. I'd appreciate it if you'd sit in on the interviews with me. I could do with someone with experience of the industry—and this station in particular—to pick up any loose ends I miss.'

Lula's insides did a strange swoopy thing. On the one hand she was ridiculously pleased he thought so highly of her opinion, but on the other, she couldn't shake the gloomy awareness that someone else taking the job meant she'd never see him again.

'Sure, I'd be happy to sit in with you.'

The atmosphere felt weirdly heavy and strained, as though all the things they weren't saying to each other were dulling the air between them.

Or maybe she was just exhausted from a week of presenting such an intensive show.

There was a long pause in which he stared intently into her eyes, before nodding. 'Thanks, Lula.'

That was the first time he'd called her Lula instead of Tallulah since she'd taken her job back and it made her feel inexplicably wretched.

'My pleasure.'

She watched him get up and walk away, dejection swirling darkly through her brain.

Why did she only ever become entangled with men that she had no future with? There had been Dan at University, who had been set on sleeping with every living female on the planet, and Scott during her late twenties, who had decided to take a job in China but leave her behind. And all the other disastrous relationships in between. No one had fit properly.

And now Tristan: businesslike, marriage averse and totally focussed on getting back to his life in Scotland.

She could never be with someone who wasn't prepared to make the ultimate commitment to her. Even if he *was* as hot as hell. She needed stability in her life, the promise of a loving, concrete future. Not one where her partner could walk away easily if the whim took him.

It was understandable that he didn't hold the sanctity of marriage in high regard if his father had made a mockery of it for him, but it was important to her to find someone on her wavelength. Someone who understood where she was coming from.

She didn't want to spend her life arguing and not feeling good enough.

Stretching back out on the sofa, she folded her forearms over her eyes, blocking out the rest of the world.

Ah well. Life went on and so would she. Just not in the same direction as Tristan.

Unfortunately.

'So, my lovely listeners, if you could wish for a special skill, what would you choose? Be as creative as you like, but let's keep it clean, okay?'

Tristan smiled as he listened to Lula's show the following Monday. Since he'd taken over the running of *Flash* he liked to make sure he was there at the radio station in time to catch her show as it went out. He enjoyed listening to her dulcet tones as she teased and titillated her audience, keeping up the rapid momentum needed to capture busy people's attention. He could see exactly why she was so popular with the listeners—she had a real skill at finding the interesting angle to a subject.

According to reports from the Broadcast Assistants there had been a huge increase in texts and tweets to the show since she'd taken over and listener numbers were already well up for the Breakfast Show.

He'd been surprised by just how much he was enjoying looking after the station too. The business he ran from Scotland was pretty dry in nature, although their turnover was substantially more than the radio station was making. Entertaining people certainly wasn't as much of a money-spinner as installing industrial kitchens and providing catering equipment to restaurants.

Still, at the end of the day, it had to be the money that mattered—it was his linchpin, the thing that kept him focussed and motivated. That kept his world turning—that made everything make sense.

As soon as Lula's show was over he caught up with her as she exited the studio.

'We have our first interviewee coming in at two o'clock. Are you okay to sit in?'

She pressed her lips into an accommodating smile, although he guessed she must be pretty exhausted after her show and desperate to get home. She was a trooper all right. He really admired that about her.

'Sure, no problem,' she said, pulling the headphones that he'd bought her from around her neck and cradling them in her hands.

He nodded at them. 'How are your headphones working out?'

She gave him her first genuine smile in days. 'They're great. I love them. Fantastic sound quality. You certainly know the way to a girl's heart.' She seemed to freeze as if realising she'd said something entirely inappropriate.

He stepped towards her, not sure exactly what he meant to do, but unable to stop himself. 'Glad to hear I haven't lost my touch,' he said with a smile, continuing the move by leaning against the wall next to her.

His stomach plummeted when she took a quick step back.

These little rejections were starting to get to him.

They reminded him of the small moves away that Marcy had started to do towards the end of their relationship.

He wished it didn't have to be this way with her, but since they'd made that pact over dinner about keeping things professional she'd been friendly, but stand-offish with him.

He could understand her reasoning for it, but that didn't mean he had to like it.

'Well, I'd better get on,' she said, raising both eyebrows and smacking her lips together. 'Don't want the boss to catch me slacking off, who knows what sort of punishment he might dish out,' she murmured in that seductive voice of hers. Flashing him a cheeky grin, she swivelled on the spot and walked off, leaving him staring after her retreating figure with a bemused smile on his face and a pressing concern in his trousers.

Okay, maybe professional and stand-offish was easier to handle.

The interview was a disaster. Tristan knew as soon as the guy walked in that he wouldn't fit the ethos of the station. He was too straight, too stuffy, too jobsworthy.

When Lula asked him some pointed questions about his vision for the station it was clear he thought she wasn't important enough to engage with and addressed all his answers to Tristan instead.

No way was he going to hand over the running of the station to such a chauvinist idiot.

'What did you think?' Lula asked after the guy left, clearly hoping he hated him as much as it sounded like she did.

'Totally wrong. No way.'

She blew out a breath and relaxed back into her chair.

'Thank God for that. I don't think I could have worked with someone who treated me as if I was invisible.'

The flash of hurt in her eyes made him want to go over and pull her against him, to wrap her up in his arms and give her the reassurance she visibly craved.

This impulse must have shown on his face because colour rushed up her neck and her gaze shot away from his and down to where her hands now gripped her thighs, as if she was fighting urges of her own.

Forcing himself to maintain a façade of cool, he flipped her a smile. 'Ah, don't let him get to you. The guy was clearly an idiot of the highest order. I suspect he's the type who feels emasculated by smart, attractive women.'

Something sparked in her eyes and she opened her mouth as if to speak, but shut it again and gave him a grateful smile instead. 'I'd better go,' she said, inclining her head towards the door. 'I've still got a tonne of research to do on a music producer I'm interviewing tomorrow.'

'Okay.' He watched her get up from the chair, wondering what was going through her head at that precise moment. If it was anything like the notions he'd been conjuring up since her 'punishment' remark there was no wonder she was finding it hard to hold it together.

'Lula,' he called out, as she reached the door, not wanting her to go yet, but aware he didn't have a good reason to ask her to stay.

She turned and faced him again, her brows drawn up in question. 'Yes?'

There was a beat of silence while he thought of something suitable to say. 'Thanks again for helping me out with the interviews. I really appreciate it.'

Her shoulders appeared to relax and she smiled, as

if she'd keyed herself up for something that now wasn't going to happen. 'It's my pleasure,' she said, before opening the door and striding purposefully away.

Despite the brief diversion into flirty banter, the next week went pretty much the same way as the previous one—with her still avoiding him as much as possible or keeping things polite and professional when she had to be in his company.

His frustration grew by the day and he found himself deliberately going out of his way to be in the same room as her or sit next to her whenever the opportunity arose just to feel her vibrate with the same tension he experienced whenever she was in his vicinity.

It gave him a perverse satisfaction to see her squirm. She was obviously feeling the same heat he was and he became more and more determined to get her to show it.

He needed to prove to himself that he wasn't the sort of guy that women—that *she*—could walk away from easily.

They interviewed two more candidates together who'd applied for the Station Manager's job, but Tristan hated both of them.

He was beginning to feel a little possessive about the station now that he was getting to know the staff better. The place had an exhilarating, ever-changing buzz about it and he was surprised to find himself less and less inclined to get back to his business in Scotland.

His second in command seemed to have everything under control there—bar a couple of things that needed Tristan's specific attention—which was both heartening and humbling. He'd always thought things there would fall apart without him, but apparently he wasn't as essential to its smooth running as he'd imagined.

When his father had handed over the running of their

business to him after he finished University, he'd felt the great weight of responsibility to their family legacy on his shoulders. He hadn't realised just how much it had consumed him until he'd stepped away from it.

Despite the minor knock to his pride when he realised he wasn't as essential there as he'd imagined, he felt lighter and freer than he had in a long time.

Working at *Flash* had been good for him.

On Friday afternoon he was finishing off the schedules for the following week when the broadcast assistant, Claire, knocked on his office door.

'Hey, Tristan, we're all going out for drinks this evening to celebrate my birthday, fancy coming along?'

He could tell from the colour on her cheeks that it had taken some courage to come and ask him. Even though he made sure to be friendly to the staff, Claire in particular still treated him with detached reverence.

He thought about it for all of two seconds. 'Sure, I'd love to.' He hadn't done any socialising with the staff since he'd started working here and he was gratified that they'd want to include him.

Perhaps Lula would be there too tonight and he'd get an opportunity to spend some time with her outside of work. Maybe he'd get her to loosen up around him in a more relaxed environment? To show some more of that spirit that bubbled underneath the surface of her control.

Memories of how they'd loosened up the last time they'd been out together flashed through his head and a sizzling heat swept through his body.

The sight of Claire's delighted smile dragged him back to the present.

'That's great! We're meeting at eight at The Zetter Townhouse cocktail bar on Clerkenwell Road. See you there later,' she said.

He raised a capitulating hand, still a little distracted by his erotic recollections. 'Sure. See you there.'

Lula stood in a cobbled square in front of a row of golden-bricked townhouses with white stucco frontages and checked the text from Claire again to make sure she'd got the right place.

To the right of her was the blue door that Claire described and next to it a discreet plaque with the name The Zetter engraved on it.

Yup, this was it.

Pushing the door open, she took a deep breath, readying herself to be sociable.

It was good for her to be here tonight. She hadn't been out since the meal with Tristan—apart from a slobby night over at Emily's place watching a film and drinking a questionable new cocktail her friend had concocted.

She'd somehow managed not to mention Tristan's ongoing existence in her life to her friend, sure she'd be in for a thorough interrogation about him, which she wasn't prepared to handle at the moment.

Quite honestly she wasn't even sure she'd have the energy to stay out for long tonight. Getting into the routine of regular early morning rising from Monday to Friday, that the Breakfast Show required, was taking longer than she'd anticipated and having to go in each day and act all cool and indifferent around Tristan wasn't doing much for the state of her nerves either.

The guy seriously knew how to rock her boat.

She seemed to spend most of her day in a state of sexual agitation and every time he came within ten feet of her, which was surprisingly often—in fact she suspected he was doing it deliberately to rattle her—she turned into a gibbering wreck.

But she was determined to put him out of her mind and have fun tonight. She deserved to raise a glass with her colleagues to her promotion as Breakfast Presenter—something she hadn't managed to find the time to do before now.

It was comfortably dim inside, the dark red walls and long bookshelves groaning with leather-bound books adding an air of stately elegance to an eclectic mash-up of vintage furniture. It felt a bit like an eccentric, rich old uncle's time capsule house.

There was already a large gathering of people lounging on purple velvet sofas, boxing in a long, low glass display case which was being used as a table. It had a random collection of old looking objects inside it: yellowing handwritten letters, brass compasses and a stuffed rabbit wearing a top hat.

The place was kooky as all heck.

Claire, as birthday girl, sat at the head of the table and Lula gave her a wave before going over to the bar to grab herself an orange and soda. If she even had a sniff of a cocktail tonight she'd be done for.

Lula located a bit of space on one of the sofas and slid into it. When she looked up from finding a place for her drink amongst the litter of cocktail glasses she was shocked to see Tristan sitting opposite her, giving her one of his killer smiles.

Her insides turned to goo.

What the heck was he doing here? Had Claire really invited their boss to her birthday do? And had he accepted knowing she'd probably be there? Not that he shouldn't be allowed to socialise with the staff, but these were *her* friends.

She experienced a rush of frustration with him for turning up and hijacking her night with his befuddling presence.

How was she meant to relax tonight and make intelligent conversation with Tristan sitting there looking like his sex god self in her peripheral vision?

She gave him a quick nod of acknowledgment and turned to talk to the man sitting next to her, doing her best to ignore him.

Tristan's pulse had given an electrified stutter when Lula appeared and slid onto the sofa opposite him, but he'd been frustrated when she'd only given him a curt nod and turned away.

Well, he wasn't going to let her get away with ignoring him all night here too.

After chatting for a while with a couple of the radio engineers from the station about who was the best live band at the moment, he disengaged himself from the conversation and covertly watched Lula over his tumbler as he sipped his Whiskey Sour. The guy sitting next to her seemed to be regaling her with a monologue that had her captivated and she didn't once glance his way, which narked him. He didn't believe she felt nothing for him any more. It wasn't possible, not after the intense connection they'd shared.

She spent a lot of time listening to people, he realised, watching as she nodded and encouraged the guy to elucidate on his point. He suspected that's what made her so good at her job.

He spent a moment sizing the guy up. He didn't recognise him from the station so by deduction he must be a friend of Claire's. Blood rushed to his head as he watched him put a hand on Lula's knee. The guy clearly thought a lot of himself, judging by the way he kept smoothing a hand over his ridiculous on-trend hairstyle and lounging across the sofa as if he owned the place.

Tristan was unnerved by how protective he felt towards Lula and how frustrated he was that she was the only person he wanted to talk to tonight and she was sitting on the other side of table being openly pawed by some cocky youth who was totally beneath her.

As he watched with narrowed eyes she stifled a yawn behind her hand and glanced round, catching his eye.

The connection between them seemed to sizzle the air as they stared at each other. She didn't need to say anything for him to know she needed him to rescue her.

Standing up, he navigated his way out of the group and round to the back of the sofa where she was sitting.

Leaning down between her and the youth, he gave her a friendly smile.

'Hey, Lula, how are you doing?'

Her pupils seemed huge in the muted light of the bar. 'Not bad, but my new boss is a bit of a slave-driver so I'm pretty wiped out.' She shot him a teasing smile, which he returned, pleased she was joking around with him again. 'I was thinking about heading off soon actually,' she continued, her gaze sliding away from his. 'Need to get an early night in.'

'Yeah? Me too. I'll walk out with you,' he said, standing up and waiting pointedly for her to do the same.

He missed the flirty banter they'd had between them and this was an ideal opportunity to get her on her own and talk freely without the worry of being interrupted or overheard.

Her look of surprise swiftly turned to apprehension. 'You don't need to do that, Tristan—'

'I know that, but I'm pretty done in too. I'll walk

you to the tube. I'm in an apartment in St Pancras now so it's on my way.'

'You're not in the hotel any more?' From the pink hue of her cheeks she was evidently thinking about the night she'd spent there with him—just as he was now. Blood roared through his veins and he shifted behind her, attempting to disguise the incongruous effect the memories were having on him.

'I thought if I was going to be here for a couple more weeks I'd be better off renting a short lease apartment. A friend of mine owns a place in the clock tower of St Pancras station.'

'Really?' She widened her eyes, her interest clearly piqued.

'Yeah, it's a great place. Good location.'

'It sure is.'

There was an awkward silence.

'Okay. Let's go,' he said, not wanting to give her an opportunity to back out.

She studied him for a few more beats.

From the way her eyelids flickered, he felt sure she was having another of those internal arguments in her head.

'Okay, that would be great,' she said finally.

After saying their goodbyes to a rather inebriated Claire, who was now happily being charmed by another of the foppish youths in the party, they exited the bar into the cool night air of the cobbled square.

'I should have made it clear we weren't leaving *together*,' Lula muttered, frowning hard at the door they'd just closed behind them.

'Want me to go back and make an announcement to the bar about how we're not going to sleep together tonight?' Tristan teased. He was gratified to see her mouth twitch into a begrudging smile.

'No!' She slapped him gently on the arm, her touch leaving an echo of sensation on his skin. 'That would *really* set tongues wagging. Protesting too much, and all that.'

He grinned, resisting the urge to bend down and kiss the pseudo scowl off her face and gestured for her to start walking.

After a couple of steps she stumbled on the cobblestones and he instinctively took her arm, feeling her tense beneath his grip, but she didn't pull away.

Her body felt warm and solid next to his and her hip bumped gently against his thigh as they walked, only increasing his desire to push her into a dark alleyway and make a mockery of his last statement.

They strolled in edgy silence as they navigated their way through the narrow cobbled back streets of Farringdon towards the tube station.

'Are you really living in the clock tower at St Pancras?' Lula finally asked.

'Uh-huh.'

'That's just so…' She searched around for the word she was after, her cheeks glowing pink with the effort to locate it.

'Pretentious?' he supplied, grinning at her growing frustration. 'Ridiculous? Showy?'

'It's just so goddamn *cool*. How do you manage to make *cool* seem so effortless?'

He snorted. 'I didn't realise I did, but thanks for the compliment.'

'You're welcome.'

'You want to see it?' he asked, fully expecting her to shoot him down, but unable to stop himself from pushing at her—craving the satisfaction of watching her break and admit she wanted more than detached politeness between them too.

She glanced his way, her eyes wide with excitement. 'I'd love to see it—if I'm not imposing on your evening too much—just a quick glance—I'll run in and out—I've always wanted to see what it's like in there,' she said, her voice breathy at the end of the run-on sentence.

Her verbiage amused him. It proved to him that he still had the desired effect on her—although she was clearly determined to establish she wasn't after anything more than a look-see of where he was living tonight.

No funny business, her expression said.

He smiled. 'No problem. I'm not planning on going out again this evening.' He wasn't making any other promises though.

'Okay then. Thanks.'

They jumped on the tube and travelled one stop to St Pancras, joining the fast moving crowds milling through the turnstiles and out onto to the main road.

Lula looked up at the majestic clock tower of the red-bricked gothic revival building and whistled. 'Nice one, Tristan, that's quite a find.'

'It helps to have friends with high places,' he quipped.

'Very droll,' she said, her eyes flashing with amusement.

He let them in through the glass-fronted entrance and they walked up to his apartment. He tried not to watch her tidy behind as she climbed in front of him on her customary heels, her hips swinging in a mesmerising motion right in his field of vision.

She had such a neat figure. So perfectly formed.

He smiled at her gasp of astonishment as he opened the front door to reveal the apartment in all its glory.

It really was magnificent, with its ten-meter-high ceilings, exposed brickwork and one whole wall dedicated to an enormous bookcase, filled with the brightly coloured spines of hundreds of books. She moved around the place, running her hands over the sleek modern furniture, the exposed beams, the wrought iron spiral staircase that led up to the mezzanine where the master bedroom was located.

When she turned back to him her eyes were bright with wonder.

'Why on earth doesn't your friend still live here? God, if I owned this place I'd never want to set foot outside, let alone allow someone else to rent it.'

'His wife wanted somewhere bigger after they got married. She made him give this place up.' He rolled his eyes skyward.

She smiled down at the floor. 'Is that a hint of disdain I detect?'

He shrugged. 'He had a good thing going here. Now he's living like a zombie in the burbs and kowtowing to a wife who barely allows him out in the evenings.'

'Hmm, definitely disdain.' She ran her fingers over the back of the sofa, her gaze focussed on the undulating motion.

He slumped down onto the sofa opposite and watched her walk around the rest of the apartment, moving into the small kitchen diner, then back out to the living area again.

She sat down on the sofa opposite and looked at him, her brows drawn up into a frown. 'You know, maybe you're different to your dad? Maybe you'll find you like the idea of getting married once you've found the right person.' There was a lilt of hope in her voice as if she couldn't bring herself to believe that he was fine as he was. What was it with the women he met? Why did they always seem to think he needed fixing?

He gave her a tolerant smile. 'Maybe, but I doubt it. I've just come out of a relationship with a woman who I thought was a perfect match for me, but I never felt the urge to marry her.'

Her face seemed pale under the bright overhead light and her gaze slid away from his. 'Why *did* you split up with your girlfriend?'

Even though he didn't want to talk to Lula about the mess his life had become, he didn't want to lie to her either. She'd asked him a direct question so he should give her a direct answer. 'She left me for my brother.'

Her mouth dropped open in surprise. 'No! That's so tacky!'

He'd expected pity, so was heartened by her outrage. He smiled, attempting to keep things light, even though his whole body was hot with discomfort. 'Yeah, tacky and humiliating.'

'I can't believe your own brother would do that to you.'

'Well, that's Jon.' He huffed out a laugh. 'It wouldn't have been so bad if I hadn't carried the bastard for so many years.'

'What do you mean?'

He frowned, realising he wasn't going to get away with just giving her vague details; she was more savvy than that. 'After our mum died, my father went to pieces so it was up to me to keep our lives on the rails. I made sure Jon had what he needed for school and that he turned up to classes.'

Lula was sitting forwards now, a look of keen interest on her face.

He leaned back against the hard back of the sofa and

rubbed a hand through his hair, strangely relieved at the prospect of getting all this off his chest. 'And then, when my dad became more interested in chasing women than running our family business I stepped in to keep it going after I finished University. I really wanted to set up my own thing, I had grand plans, but I couldn't see the business that had been in my family for fifty years sold off or go to ruin. My brother said he'd help me with the running of it, but he hardly ever turns up for work. He has no qualms about taking his wage and dividends though. And then stealing my girlfriend out from under my nose.'

She was looking at him with such incredulous indignation he almost reached forward to touch her in gratitude.

The air between them throbbed with tension as they stared at each other in the pause.

She broke eye contact first and smoothed her skirt down over her legs.

He bristled as he realised he must have made her uncomfortable by treating her like a sounding board.

'Hey, I need to ask you something,' he said, standing up and walking over to the bookcase to straighten one of the spines, giving her a moment of grace. He'd got too personal and she was evidently struggling with how to respond to his embarrassing admission.

'Apparently there's a Radio Industry networking event next Thursday, which Jez was meant to be attending. It's a good opportunity to shout about *Flash* and maybe sniff out some more sponsorship. Assuming I haven't found anyone to take over managing the station by then, I'd appreciate it if you'd come along with me. I could do with an expert on hand to deal with the specific radio industry questions.'

When he glanced back she was frowning. Was it because she didn't want to have to spend another evening in his company? Had he blown his *cool* image by telling her all his dirty secrets?

The thought irked him, which is why his next question came out sounding so accusatory. 'Surely you anticipated there'd be some out of hours demands on your time?'

She nodded, her eyes big with distress. 'Yes, of course.'

From the tone of her voice you'd have thought he'd asked her to perform an operatic duet in top F with him. Or maybe she just felt uncomfortable about being seen on his arm.

'Look, we don't have to go for long and I'll make sure I mention to everyone we speak to that you're not sleeping with the boss.' He gave her a jokey raised-eyebrow-and-smile combo.

She barely broke a grin back.

Hmm, perhaps it *was* inappropriate to keep making those kind of jokes. His heart sank in his chest. He'd been enjoying clowning around with her this evening and elated by how close they were to stepping over the line she'd drawn, but clearly it was time to get serious now.

He walked over to her sofa and sat on the arm. 'Look, I need to be honest with you, Lula. The station needs more sponsorship if it's going to survive. Jez has pretty much bled the reserves dry and it's going to take a serious injection of cash to keep it viable.' The look of shock on her face made his stomach turn over. 'I'm sorry to have to tell you like this, I never thought it would take this long to find someone to take over the managerial position. I was expecting they'd be the one to tackle the problem of the financial shortfall.'

Her face had taken on a ghostly white pallor. 'I had no idea things were so bad.'

He held up a placating hand. 'It's salvageable. But we need to put on a confident outward appearance or the sponsors will start getting worried that they're backing a dead duck.'

Lula drew her shoulders back and her chin up. 'I'd be happy to go with you and represent *Flash*. I'll do whatever it takes to keep the station running,' she said, her voice now dynamic and businesslike. 'I love that place. It's got the potential to grow into something amazing. I couldn't bear to see it die a death.'

The panic in her eyes propelled him forwards off the arm and onto the cushion next to her and he put a reassuring hand on her arm.

She glanced down at where his fingers pressed against her soft skin, then back into his face, her eyes wide and dazed.

They stared at each other, their bodies closer than they'd been since that fateful night. His blood raged through his veins and he became acutely aware of how hard he was, how easy it would be to push her down onto the sofa and kiss her, how much he wanted to be inside her.

'I'd better get going and leave you to the rest of your evening,' she murmured, the breathiness of her voice doing crazy things to him.

Before he could respond, she stood up and spun on her heels, walking quickly away from him towards the door. Pulling it open, she stepped out into the hallway. She paused and turned back, fixing him with a tight smile. 'Thanks for letting me see your place, it's amazing.'

He had a sudden wild urge to ask her to stay, to try to reassure her that everything would be okay if she did, but before the words would come out of his mouth she'd turned and walked away.

CHAPTER SEVEN

'GOOD GRIEF, LULA, you look awful. Please tell me it's down to a wild night with a hawt man.'

'Not exactly.' Lula gave Emily a pained smile as she dropped into the hard wooden café seat opposite her.

They were having their customary Saturday brunch in a little place in Crouch End they'd frequented since meeting at UCL, whilst doing a Media Studies degree together.

Emily took a bite of the cinnamon swirl the waitress had just placed in front of her and raised a questioning eyebrow, waiting for Lula to spill the beans.

'Hold up, let me order some carbs and caffeine first,' Lula said, giving the waitress a grateful smile as she waited patiently for her to choose what she wanted. 'I barely slept last night and my brain isn't functioning yet.' She placed an order for a bran muffin and a large Americano and slumped back in her chair, only to find her friend glaring at her, impatient for gossip.

Lula sighed. There was no way she was going to get away with keeping Tristan's continued existence in her life from Emily. Her friend had a way of sniffing out trouble and strife. 'It's a long story, Em.'

'I have all the time in the world right now,' Em said,

taking a sip of her café latte and gesturing for Lula to continue.

So she started at the point where Emily had left her with Tristan in the pub and filled in the blanks up till the present, her heart racing and her whole body so tightly wound she thought she might break into a million pieces if anyone so much as touched her.

'Whoa,' Emily said as Lula ended her monologue by describing the unnervingly intense dream she'd had in the early hours about walking around Tristan's flat naked while he looked down on her from the mezzanine.

'No wonder you look so frazzled. That's some serious sexual frustration you're dealing with,' Emily said, flipping her a grin.

Lula put her head in her hands. 'I'm an idiot, pure and simple. What the hell was I thinking, agreeing to go back to his flat? I've just made everything so much worse.'

'Maybe, subconsciously, you were hoping something would happen?' Emily said, making it clear in her tone that was exactly what she believed.

Lula nodded into her hands. 'I told myself at the time that I wanted to see this amazing place he was staying in—and I did—but that wasn't really it.'

'Clearly.'

Lula raised her head and gave her friend a sorrowful grimace. 'I wish I didn't know all those personal details about him—especially about his evil ex-girlfriend leaving him for his lazy brother. It makes it so much harder to be indifferent when he makes me *care* about him like that.'

'Understandable.'

'I came so close to leaning forwards and kissing him,

Em. When he touched my arm it felt like my whole body exploded into this big fiery ball of need. It took everything I had to stand up and walk out of there.'

'Why *did* you walk? I wouldn't have done. I'd have got my rocks off and left a satisfied woman.'

Lula snorted. That was just like her friend. 'I don't have the ability to keep things unemotional like you.'

'It's not about being unemotional,' Emily said tartly, 'It's about putting yourself first for once.'

'And look what happened when I tried that before. I've been pretending to be someone I'm not the whole time I've been around him. I think he believes I'm actually like *Louise*. If he found out I'm not really like that he'd lose interest pretty damn quickly.'

Emily twisted her mouth into a grim smile. 'Don't be daft, Lu.'

'It always seems to happen though, Em. As soon as I relax and start being myself they lose interest in me.'

'That's because you're picking the wrong men and expecting too much of them. You've got this crazy idea that there's some perfect individual out there, but there isn't, Lu. Everyone's messed up in their own sweet way. To be blunt, you're living in a dream world if you think you're going to find someone who you can absolutely guarantee will never leave you. Most of the men I've met are only out for themselves.'

'Tristan isn't like that.' Her tone came out snappier than she intended and Emily gave her a knowing smile.

'Then maybe it's worth giving it a go with him?'

She shook her head. 'I don't think he'd respond too well to me telling him I've been pretending to be this confident, outgoing woman the whole time. Look how quickly he shut me down when he thought I'd been using him to keep my job.'

'Yeah, well, I guess being dumped for his brother has to have had an impact on his self-confidence. It's not surprising he's so paranoid. Not that it sounds like he exactly fought you off that night. The dawg.' Emily wiggled her eyebrows and gave one of her show-stopping smiles.

Lula couldn't rustle up a return smile this time. 'He did seem to be genuinely into me. At least I thought so at the time.'

'And he's definitely not interested in a relationship now?'

She shook her head. 'Nope. He's made it pretty clear he's heading back up to Scotland as soon as he's found a new Station Manager.'

'And your reasoning for not having a hot fling in the meantime is…?'

'If anyone at the station found out I was sleeping with him my credibility would be less than zero. It was awful when everyone found out about Jez.'

'That's because *Jez* was awful.'

Lula gave her friend a pained look and took a sip of her drink.

'He was a smarmy little twonk, Lu.'

She nearly snorted coffee out of her nose. 'Nice insult.'

Emily frowned. 'Lula, the only person who thinks you don't deserve to be happy is you. Your bloody parents have a lot to answer for,' she said, swiping some crumbs from her muffin off the table, her expression unusually serious. It wasn't like Emily to get heavy with the semantics and it brought Lula up short. Tears pressed at the back of her eyes and she took another long sip of coffee to cover her loss of cool.

Another horrible thought struck her. 'He's probably

still in love with his ex-girlfriend anyway. He told me he'd thought she was the perfect woman for him. There's no way I want to get caught up in a rebound thing and then left behind when he's had enough.'

'I hear you,' Emily said, polishing off her coffee and motioning for the waitress to bring her another one.

'The last thing I need is to fall for my boss right now,' Lula continued, warming to her theme now. 'I should be putting all my energy into making a success of my Breakfast Show, not mooning around after someone who doesn't give a fig about me.'

Emily was looking at her with a baffled expression. 'If you say so.'

'I do,' Lula said resolutely, picking up her muffin and taking a large bite.

She was putting Tristan out of her mind once and for all. From now on her energy was going into working and friends only; everything else would have to take a back seat.

After spending Saturday morning in a state of restless sexual frustration, Tristan called up a couple of old Uni friends and arranged to meet up with them over the weekend. He needed a distraction from the slow, sinking feeling that he'd made a total balls-up of his last interaction with Lula.

She seemed to be able to wreck his hard-worked-for control with just the glimmer of a smile and it made him jumpy.

'You okay, Tristan? Something on your mind?' his friend Alex asked as they stared out across the spectacular view of the city from the top of the London Eye.

'Just work stuff,' Tristan replied, unwilling to get into the whole mess with Lula. He couldn't even get how he felt about her straight in his own head, let alone explain it to someone else.

'Business okay in Scotland?'

He nodded at his friend. 'Fine. Same as usual, but it's good to have a break from it, to be honest.'

'Was it right after Uni when you took over there?'

'Yeah. Ten years ago now.'

He was actually shocked to realise it had been that long. No wonder he was feeling jaded about going back to it. Being at the radio station had made such a refreshing change.

'Didn't you used to have some great schemes and plans for setting up something by yourself? I thought the idea was only to learn the ropes at the family business, then move on.'

Tristan sighed. 'It was, but I got stuck there. My dad totally lost interest in it and my brother doesn't give a toss about it either, so I stayed. It's been good though. It's a profitable business.'

'But dull as hell?'

'Yeah. It's not the most scintillating industry to be in, but it pays well.'

'Fair dos,' Alex said, before he was distracted by his two-year-old daughter and dragged away to look at a view from the other side of the pod.

Tristan watched him interacting with his kid and felt a strange sense of longing that he'd not experienced before. Lula's face flashed into his mind, but he boxed it, knowing it was ridiculous to read more into his connection with her than was actually there. He was just tired and out of his comfort zone and it was making him feel sentimental.

They wanted very different things and it would be crazy to believe otherwise.

* * *

After a few more days of keeping her head down and disappearing whenever Tristan walked into the room, Lula was ready to face the Radio Industry networking event with her calm restored.

Sort of.

Her nerves weren't just about having to maintain a state of emotional distance from Tristan all night, though, the thought of performing as her DJ persona face to face with all those people made her feel positively queasy.

She'd never been good at socialising in large parties. The mere thought of having to make small talk with total strangers without the anonymity of her microphone and a closed studio made her jittery, but she knew she had to suck it up and put on a good show if they were going to persuade more companies to invest in the station.

The success of *Flash* had to be her main priority here.

Tristan finally caught up with her after her show, the day of the networking event.

'Are you still on for tonight?' he said, blocking her way out of the studio so she was forced to stop and talk to him.

It was the first time she'd been this close to him since the night in his apartment and her body trembled with tension as she attempted to stay cool and collected in the face of his intense charisma.

'Yes, I'm all keyed up and ready to go.' She gave him the most assertive smile she could manage.

The sexual hunger in his returning grin made heat rush straight between her thighs.

His reaction only reinforced her assertion that it was

fabricated 'self-assured Lula' that he was attracted to though.

'Great. Well, the thing starts at eight, so I'll pick you up in a cab at seven-thirty,' he said moving closer.

She put up a hand, her heart thumping hard. 'No, that's okay. I'll just meet you there.'

His brow creased in confusion. 'It's no trouble, Lula.'

'I know, but I'd rather make my own way there, thanks.' She'd stood firm, knowing if she had to spend any time with him in the close confines of a car she was bound to start the evening a flustered mess. There'd be plenty of time for her to degenerate into a tangle of nerves once they were there.

After scanning her face, he finally nodded. 'Okay, if that's what you'd prefer.'

'I would prefer that, yes.'

She almost bit the words back as she registered his offended expression, but before she could open her mouth to try and explain, he'd turned around and strode away.

As promised, Tristan waited for Lula outside the revolving doors to the imposing Mandarin Oriental hotel in Knightsbridge.

All the breath left his lungs as he watched her walk up the steps to where he stood. She looked utterly beautiful in a figure-hugging, sleeveless gold dress that clung to her amazing curves and stopped just above her knees displaying a pair of gold six-inch-heel shoes. She could have been the goddess of opulence with her long hair piled loosely on top of her head and her bright eyes sparkling with metallic-coloured make-up.

No one was going to treat her as if she was invisible tonight.

His gut twisted as he remembered how cold she'd been towards him earlier that afternoon, no, strike that, since she'd walked out of his apartment the previous Friday night.

She'd very obviously been avoiding him since then and he didn't like it one bit. This need to push and push for a reaction had become something of an obsession for him and the constant knock-backs were beginning to get to him.

He really respected her assertiveness though. She was the bravest, most electrifying woman he'd ever met and he wanted her. More than he'd wanted anyone or anything in his life before. But most of all, he wanted her to admit she wanted him back.

'Hey,' he said as she reached the top of the steps. 'You look beautiful.'

Her gaze didn't quite meet his and he wondered whether she considered *beautiful* to be an inappropriate word to use. Admittedly, it wasn't usually utilised in the boss/employee vocabulary but it fitted the context perfectly.

'Thanks,' she murmured in that sexually evocative voice of hers and he wondered how he was going to get through the evening when all he wanted to do was drag her off to bed and do wicked things to her.

They walked through the glossy marble lobby to the cocktail bar, which was already thronging with people. It was an impressive place. The right hand wall was made up of glass cabinets displaying a dazzling array of cocktail glasses and an impressive range of wine bottles. The rest of the place was done out in brown leather, glass and chrome with a long catwalk-shaped bar in the centre of the room.

When he glanced at her, Tristan was surprised to see Lula hanging back with a fixed smile on her face.

Okay, time for a drink.

After grabbing two glasses of red wine from a passing waiter he handed one to Lula. 'Shall we mingle?' he said.

She nodded, then held up one finger and took a long sip of her wine, before flashing him a steady smile. 'Let's do it.'

Resisting the urge to put a guiding hand at the base of her back, he walked around the room with her, dropping in and out of conversations, which Lula let him lead, adding in her own words of wisdom as necessary.

He could tell people were impressed with her and he felt a surge of pride to be there in her company. Quite a few mentioned they'd heard her show recently and complimented her on it. She accepted the praise with a gratified smile, but Tristan was concerned by how subdued she seemed otherwise.

Surely she couldn't be that uncomfortable in his company?

She nipped out a couple of times for a bathroom break and he found each time that he felt hollow without her there by his side and relieved when she returned to stand with him again.

As they were chatting with a small group of people that worked at one of the other independent stations in the region they were approached by a guy wearing a loud shirt and a big smile. He zeroed in on Lula and began talking to her about how his company was looking to run some ads on one of the younger, more cutting-edge radio stations.

'I have to say, your weekday Breakfast Show is markedly better than it used to be when Jez was presenting.' He leaned in conspiratorially. 'The guy's a good businessman, but he's a little *parochial* when it comes to DJing. Better to leave the presenting to the talent, I say.' He gave Lula a knowing wink.

She smiled pleasantly but didn't say anything back.

Tristan jumped in quickly and pressed the guy to talk more about his needs—hyper-aware that they had to grab any lead they could right now.

He chatted for a while to the guy and managed to arrange for him to come to the station the following week and have a chat about buying some targeted airtime.

After he moved on, Tristan turned back to Lula to give her a furtive high-five, but she was staring round the bar as if in a daze.

'Lula? You okay?'

'I'm just going to the bathroom,' she said, giving him a firm smile.

'Again?' He pinched his brows together in concern. Was she ill? When he looked carefully he realised she did seem a bit paler than usual.

'What, is there a limit on bathroom breaks or something?' she said, jokily, although the wild look in her eyes told him to back off. He didn't want to though, not until he was sure she was okay.

'No, of course not.' He was concerned to see she was trembling. 'I'll come with you,' he said, gesturing out of the bar.

She twitched her eyebrow into an expression that said *Why would you want to visit the ladies' toilet with me?*

'Not to the bathroom,' he clarified with a grin. 'Just out of here.'

Lula walked quickly out of the bar with Tristan hot on her heels.

She needed some head space, away from all these

people. It was great they all seemed to want to talk to her, but her reserves for intelligent banter were quickly depleting and she could only stand there mute for so long, allowing Tristan to lead the conversation, before it began to look like she wasn't making an effort.

And it wasn't just the fact she felt she was making a mess of selling herself and the station, but that she was doing it standing next to a man who only had to glance her way to turn her brain to jelly. She was finding it virtually impossible to concentrate without being distracted by Tristan's intoxicating scent and the sexual magnetism that seemed to roll off him in waves.

Her body actually felt feverish with arousal.

She must be coming across as a real idiot tonight and she really didn't want him to think badly of her.

She made her way down the corridor towards the bathrooms with Tristan one step behind, her body burning with awareness of his presence in the cool quiet.

'See you in a sec,' she said, pushing the door open and striding inside before he could answer her.

Pressing her forehead against the cold glass of the full-length mirror next to the sinks, she took some deep breaths, willing her mind to clear and her heart-rate to slow down.

This was torture. Added to the strain of dealing with being around Tristan, the event itself was bringing back memories of the awful parties her parents used to hold where she was expected to circulate, making witty, intelligent conversation with their friends, when all she wanted to do was run away and hide. She used to feel physically sick before them—and sometimes tried to convince her parents that she actually *was* ill. They never let her off them though. Apparently they thought it was imperative for her to learn how to act in polite company. She'd never been able to get it right, always managing to say the wrong thing to someone and chastising herself for days, or sometimes weeks, afterwards.

This networking thing was bringing back all those old feelings of insecurity she'd fought to get past.

'Are you okay? You looked like you were about to pass out in there,' he said as soon as she exited the bathrooms and found him leaning against the wall, waiting for her.

'I'm fine.'

He put a hand on her arm to stop her walking past him and as she turned to face him, he gave her a puzzled look. 'Are you sure?'

His concern seemed to make everything so much worse. She threw up her hands, humiliation making her face burn. 'What do you want from me, Tristan? I said I'm okay. Let's just get back in there and get this thing over with.'

He gave her a puzzled grimace. 'You make it sound like a trial.'

Her gaze slid away from his. 'Well, it is a bit, isn't it? Having to make small talk with all those people, hoping they'll throw some benevolence our way. It just makes me uncomfortable, that's all.'

'I would have thought you'd enjoy being lauded as one of the brightest and best presenters in the land.'

She looked directly at him now. 'Yeah, well, you don't know me, do you?'

Damn him. Even the crinkles at the corners of his eyes when he frowned were sexy.

'Lula, what's going on?'

'What do you mean?'

'I mean why are you acting like I've killed your kitten? I know things have been awkward between us, but I don't think I deserve this sort of treatment.'

Her shoulders slumped as all the misplaced anger rushed out of her. He had a point, she was taking out her frustration on him and it wasn't fair. In fact it was downright unprofessional.

'You're right. I'm sorry.'

They heard voices coming from the other end of the corridor and she straightened her posture, steeling herself for making more polite conversation.

Tristan tore his troubled gaze away from her to scan the corridor.

'Quick, let's nip in here.' He strode forwards a couple paces and pulled open a door to their right, ushering her in.

She caught the flash of grim determination on his face before he closed the door behind them, leaving them standing in the dark.

'Tristan, we're in a broom cupboard.'

'Yeah, I know, but at least no one will think to look for us in here.'

She couldn't help but giggle. 'They wouldn't be able to see us even if they did—it's pitch black.'

'There must be a light switch around here somewhere.'

She felt him bump into her as he groped around the walls.

'Ouch! That was my toe!' she said, as one of his feet landed on hers.

'Sorry.'

He didn't sound sorry. He sounded amused.

'It's no good, I can't find it.' The gentle rush of words right next to her ear made her realise he was standing right in front of her, only inches away.

Her heart thumped hard against her ribcage and her whole body tingled with awareness at his close proximity.

'We probably don't need light anyway. Considering you've barely looked at me tonight it's not going to make a lot of difference.' His voice was light, but she detected a twang of indignation, which made her stomach dip with guilt. 'Are you going to tell me what's wrong?' he said earnestly now.

There was nothing for it, she was going to have to lay everything on the line; they couldn't carry on like this, pretending everything was just fine and dandy.

She took a deep breath. 'To be honest, Tristan, I've been worried about keeping up the "Hotshot Tallulah Lazenby" act here. I didn't want to let you and the station down.'

'What are you talking about?' He sounded utterly confused.

Despite the humiliation burning up her neck to her face she kept going, wanting to get it all out before she lost her nerve.

'The thing is, the Lula you think you know doesn't exist. I'm nothing like my on-air personality. The "me" that you saw that night in your hotel room was a fabrication. I was playing a game, pretending to be the person I project for the radio. And once I'd started playing that part for you I felt like I couldn't drop the act in case you changed your mind about giving me the Breakfast Show. I'm just not like that. I'm shy. I like reading and quiet nights in and hiding in a crowd instead of being the centre of attention.'

There was a pause, then he sighed and the air around them moved as if he'd adjusted his position

An intense longing for him to touch her twisted her insides.

'I'm sorry I asked to you come to this awful thing,' he murmured. 'I didn't realise you hated networking so much.' He was standing so close now she could feel the heat radiating from him.

She pulled a face then chuckled, realising he couldn't see her. She was glad he hadn't found the light switch though, it was amazing how much easier it was to talk about this in the dark.

'It's okay. It's *my* problem. I've always been shy. I was the quiet kid at school who never raised her hand or spoke out, but it got to the point where I felt so invisible I realised I had to do something about it. So now I pretend to be confident and vivacious and somehow it works and everyone believes me. I still get terrified during social situations though. I'm afraid I'll have one of my brain freeze moments where I'm totally lost for words and end up staring at the person I'm talking to with a gormless look on my face. Do you ever get that?'

He laughed quietly. 'Nope. In case you hadn't noticed, I'm the sort of person you can't shut up at these things. I guess you're an off the scale introvert to my off the scale extrovert.' The warmth of his tone penetrated the darkness.

Her heart beat faster as his words sunk in. 'Is that what you think it is? Introversion?'

He moved again and her insides dipped with disappointment when she realised he must have leant back against the wall opposite her because his voice sounded a bit further away when he spoke. 'Yeah, that would be my layman's diagnosis. I had a psychologist come into the business when some of the staff weren't getting on well together and she explained how an extrovert needs to socialise and have people around them to recharge and an introvert needs alone time and quiet. Just like you do after your show. You hide away while the rest of the team—the extroverts—ride the buzz of performing together. The brain freeze thing is synonymous with introversion too. It's not a bad thing to be an introvert, in fact a business needs a few deep thinkers, you just naturally deal with situations in a more measured way.'

'Huh.' She never considered her need to retreat and hide after a show or party was so normal it had a name. She'd thought it was crippling shyness or an inability to deal with the pressure of performing. Something negative, anyway.

'I just assumed I was shy because my parents always told me I was. They found it really difficult having a daughter with limited social skills when they were both so gregarious. They ended up speaking *for* me most of the time to breach the awkward silences.'

'And look at you now, presenting the toughest show at one of the best radio stations in London.'

She huffed out a laugh. 'Yeah, I'm not quite sure how that happened.'

'Through sheer hard work and determination.' From the tone of his voice she could tell he was impressed by the success she'd made for herself. Her face glowed with gratified heat this time and once again she was grateful for the darkness.

'Yeah, well...I did a Media degree but I never expected to like DJing so much. I always assumed I'd do something behind the scenes, but it helped me find my voice. I love the anonymity of radio and I guess I use that as a bit of a crutch.'

His presence, so close yet still not touching her, made the air around them throb with tension. She felt she could probably reach out and grab hold of it if she wanted.

'You know, I'm really touched you agreed to come with me, considering you find this kind of event so tough.' He took a breath. 'I actually thought you were reluctant to come because you didn't want to be here with *me* after what I told you about my family...and things,' he said, his voice gruff and low, as if he was experiencing the exact same edgy tension in the atmosphere that she was.

'No. That really wasn't the reason.' The words caught in her mouth as she felt him move closer again and his heat and delectable scent washed over her. 'I came because you needed me.'

She realised as the words left her mouth that that *was* why she was here. She wanted the station to succeed, of course she did, but she also wanted to help Tristan in any way she could. Because she liked him.

Maybe more than liked.

There was a loaded pause before he responded. 'I did need you.' A breath. 'I do.'

The air seemed to crackle and the next second his hands found her face and slid along her jaw, drawing her towards him, and then his mouth was on hers, hot and firm and oh, so welcome.

He was kissing her like he couldn't get enough of her, running his hands possessively down her throat to skim over her shoulders and down over the swell of her breasts, his thumbs catching on her suddenly erect nipples which pushed against the tight-fitting dress she'd worn for him.

'Tristan—' she muttered against his mouth.

He drew back enough to let her speak.

'What are we doing? This is crazy.'

His hands tightened around her waist and he pulled her hard against him so she could feel how turned on he was.

'I know. I know.' His voice was guttural, strained.

He dropped kisses along her jawline, sending great twists of erotic sensation through her whole body. 'Don't think,' he murmured, the vibration of his words tickling and teasing the hypersensitive skin of her neck as he moved lower. 'Just do.'

She moaned low in her throat, suddenly totally unable to remember why she shouldn't be doing this with him. It felt so right. So good.

Sliding her hands up from his body, she cupped his face in her hands and kissed him hard and covetously, her tongue sliding firmly against his, the untameable response making her whole body throb with need.

He slammed against her, forcing her back against the wall, sending what sounded like brooms crashing to the floor.

The mood changed in the space of a second.

This wasn't playful any more; it was hot and heavy and serious.

Inevitable.

It was what she wanted. What she'd *needed* since he was last inside her.

In a shocking moment of clarity she realised that this was always going to happen.

She'd been kidding herself this whole time.

CHAPTER EIGHT

TRISTAN GROANED WITH relief as Lula wrenched his trousers open and slid a hot hand down his stomach and into his boxers, freeing him from the confines of his clothes. He was hard and so ready for her touch as she ran her fingers possessively over him.

He'd been dying to drag her away and keep her all to himself all evening and when she'd told him she was *here for him* he'd totally lost his grip on control.

He'd needed to hear that. That he wasn't on his own. That someone else cared about him. That *she* cared about him.

This growing need for her had been driving him crazy for the last couple of weeks and all his frustration came flooding out as he pressed himself into her, kissing her so hard he worried for a second he might be hurting her.

Drawing back, he cupped her face again and felt her ragged breath on his skin.

'Don't stop,' she murmured, in that taunting, husky voice of hers.

He was lost. Totally and utterly gone.

Dropping his hands from her face, he found the hem of her dress and pushed it roughly up her body then located the top of her skimpy knickers, which he skimmed down her legs, exposing her fully to his roving fingers.

She let out a gasp of pleasure as he pressed his index finger between her folds, catching the swollen nub of her clitoris with his fingertip and stroking her there for a few beats, before sliding it into her slick waiting heat.

His body gave a throb of pleasure as he realised she was as ready for this as he was.

And this was no time for finesse; he just needed to be inside her.

Right now.

'Please tell me you have a condom,' she muttered.

He stilled as the terrible truth hit him.

He didn't have one on him.

'I was hoping *you* might have brought some. Maybe hidden them about your person?' he said, his voice ragged with hope.

Despite the intensity of the moment she giggled. 'In this dress? I can barely fit my body into it.'

He groaned, low in his throat. 'I noticed. And stop talking about your body, I'm going crazy here.'

She laughed again, and he felt the tremor of the movement against his other hand, which was pressed to the bottom of her ribcage.

Leaning his forehead against hers, he slipped his hands away from her and she moaned in protest.

'Let's get out of here and go back to my apartment,' he said, taking a step backwards so he could stoop down and locate her knickers on the floor.

Don't say no, Lula, please *don't say no.*

'Okay.' Her voice was firm and true and he felt a surge of joy that her urge to carry this on hadn't been destroyed by the coitus interruptus.

'Can I have my knickers back?' she asked breathily.

'Nope. I'm keeping these,' he said, stuffing them into his pocket. He had no intention of letting her cover herself up again. He wanted to keep her pressed right up to the cliff-edge of desire, to tease her like she'd been unknowingly teasing him all evening.

There was a pause, then a gentle snort of amusement and he felt the air move as she pulled down her dress.

After quickly doing up his own clothes, he managed to locate the door handle and opened the door, squinting into the bright light of the deserted corridor.

'The coast's clear,' he said, turning back to give her a grin. He felt like a naughty schoolkid.

She looked flushed and dishevelled as she emerged from the darkness. It had to be the sexiest thing he'd ever seen in his life.

His erection pressed hard against his trousers and he pulled his jacket closed and did up the button in the hope it would go some way to disguising how turned on he was, should they have the misfortune to bump into someone on their way out.

He had to get them out of there, right now.

Grabbing her hand, he led her down the corridor and straight through the lobby and out into the cool night air, holding up a hand to stop a passing cab, which mercifully screeched to a halt for them.

It was meant to be.

Once they'd clambered into the cab and he'd given the driver his address, he pulled her hard against him, drawing her legs over his and sliding a hand between her thighs to find the naked damp heat of her again. He kissed her hard, his tongue exploring every delicious inch of her mouth while his fingers probed and slid inside her, intent on taking her right back to the edge of madness they'd achieved in the broom cupboard.

A hot and maddening ten minutes later they pulled up outside the entrance to his apartment and he passed the driver twenty pounds, and not waiting for change, pulled her out of the cab with him. He noticed with glee how she struggled to pull down her dress and gave him a look of pure filthy longing as she righted herself on her heels.

'Come on,' he said, grasping her hand and leading her into the lobby of his building.

Taking one look at her in her tight dress and heels, he scooped her up into his arms and mounted the stairs.

She squeaked in protest.

'Can't wait,' he muttered, taking two stairs at a time in his hurry.

After somehow managing to get the door open with trembling hands, he pushed her inside his apartment and kissed her again, slamming her against the wall behind them.

Their movements were frantic now as they pulled off their shoes and he tore the shirt away from his body.

'Where are your condoms?' she asked breathlessly.

'Bedroom. In the mezzanine.'

She broke away from him and walked quickly towards it, but he wasn't finished kissing her yet.

Catching hold of her arm, he spun her around and brought his mouth down onto hers again, walking her backwards towards the spiral staircase as he did so. He grasped the hem of her dress and slid it up her body, pausing while she reached round to undo a zip at one side of it so he was free to pull it over her head, leaving her totally naked.

They reached the staircase and he kissed her again, guiding her backwards onto the first step, then up another and another until they were halfway up, the exposed heat of her bleeding into him in tormenting waves.

'It's no good,' he said, breaking the kiss, 'I have to get my mouth on that amazing body of yours right now.'

She let out an approving moan and perched her behind on one of the steps, her body giving a shiver. 'Cold,' she muttered, but it didn't stop her from leaning further back, giving him the access he craved.

Dropping his head, he kissed down her body, teasing his lips and tongue over her breasts, nipping at the hard peaks of her nipples, then down her stomach to his ultimate goal between her spread thighs.

She groaned with pleasure, her breath coming out in short pants as he pulsed his tongue against her there and she arched her back, raising her hips to press harder against him. He slid his fingers easily into her again, delighting in her wild arousal as she let out a small whimper of need.

'Tristan—'

He knew what she wanted. He wanted it too.

Drawing away from her, he scooped a hand behind her back and urged her to climb the steps again, grinning at her shock and awe as her legs wobbled beneath her, barely able to hold her up any more.

'Look what you've done to me,' she gasped, a wide delighted grin spread across her face.

'You ain't seen nothing yet,' he growled, giving her a wicked smile back.

She made it to the top of the steps with his help and he lifted her into his arms, walked the two paces to the bed and dropped her onto it.

After locating a condom from a drawer in the bedside table, he discarded the rest of his clothes, sheathed himself with the latex and joined her on the bed, pushing between her thighs and kissing her swollen mouth hard.

She gasped as he entered her and he paused, worried he might have been too fast and rough and hurt her.

'Don't stop moving,' she begged, her eyes wild and intense. 'Don't you dare!'

This was the moment he'd been fantasising about since she'd left him frustrated and alone in his hotel bed and he thrust into her, his unfulfilled need for her driving him on. She rode the movement with him, digging her fingers into his upper arms and raising her hips to meet his drives.

Their kissing was frantic, their tongues and teeth clashing untidily with the force of their pent-up desire.

He was so close, so close to losing it. He had to slow things down or he'd streak ahead of her and this would all be over too soon.

Wrapping his arms around her, he rolled to one side—somehow managing to keep them connected as he pulled her with him—so she was now sitting astride him.

'Nice moves,' she gasped, her eyes wide with surprise.

He smiled back, grateful for the small break to get himself under control before she started moving again. He wanted to see her come, to know he'd driven her to the point where she'd powered through her reticence and was letting him see her at her most vulnerable.

That she trusted him.

It didn't take her long to reach her climax in this position and he held her as her body shuddered through the orgasm, her breath hot and fast on his skin as she buried her face against his neck.

A sense of overwhelming elation rushed through

him as she held him tightly in a possessive grip. Like she didn't want to let him go.

It made his heart beat faster.

He gave her a few moments to pull herself together before flipping her onto her back again and losing himself in the hot tightness of her body. She wrapped her legs round his back and urged him on, bringing her head up to kiss him as he came, shuddering with relief as all the tension he'd been bottling up poured out of him.

They lay quietly together afterwards, their limbs tangled around each other, and he experienced a sense of peace he'd not felt in a very long time.

She was good for him, like nothing else on earth that he'd found. Not work, not friends, not money.

This. Just this.

Her quiet and calm and gentleness. Like a harbour in the storm of his life.

'Why did you run away so quickly after we spent that first night together?' he asked quietly into her hair.

Pulling her head away from where it nestled against his shoulder, she gave him an artificially stern look. 'It wasn't because I wanted to keep you in a state of sexual fervour so I could manipulate you the next morning.'

He smiled back and tipped his head in a show of regret. 'Yeah, I know that now.'

'I would never do anything like that. I do have *some* integrity, you know.' She untangled her legs from his and he felt the distance she'd created between them keenly.

'I know, I know and I'm sorry for accusing you of it. I've been feeing a bit…messed up…about Marcy leaving me and it affected my reasoning.'

There was an awkward pause where he wished he could take that confession back.

'How long did you say you were together?' she asked finally, not looking him in the eye.

'Four years.'

She didn't respond to that and he sensed it was time to lighten the mood before she fell too heavily into her thoughts. There was no greater mood killer than talking about exes.

'Who'd have thought the night would end this way. This is much more fun than schmoozing with rivals and sponsors.' Finding her leg with his hand, he drew it back over his body and kissed along her jaw, running his tongue along the underside to make her shiver.

To his disappointment she stiffened instead.

'I don't want anyone at *Flash* to know about us,' she said, her voice muffled and strained.

Flopping back against his pillow, he ran a hand over his forehead. 'You're uncomfortable about shagging the boss?' He said it jokingly, but knew it would be obvious from a trip in his voice that her apprehension bothered him.

'It's just…it could make things really awkward for me there. I don't want anyone thinking I got my promotion because we're sleeping together.'

'They wouldn't think that, they all hold you in very high esteem. You should have seen how they reacted after I fired you, I didn't think I'd make it out alive at one point.'

Her brow furrowed. 'Really?'

'Yes.' He kissed her again, sliding his hand along her side and round to her pert backside, feeling her shiver with desire under his touch.

He loved how she reacted to him, as if she had no control over herself.

'I should go,' she murmured.

He tensed instinctively, increasing his grip on her. No way was he letting her leave right now, not when they'd only just breached their divide.

'Tough luck, Tallulah, you're not going anywhere for a while,' he said, rolling her onto her back and trapping her beneath him.

His heart lifted as he felt her relax and heard her delighted sigh.

'I was hoping you might say that.'

CHAPTER NINE

LULA WOKE IN the dark to the sound of running water.

As the fug of sleep lifted, memories from the night before flooded back and adrenalin spiked her blood as she realised she was still at Tristan's place.

Heart in her throat, she turned to stare at the brightly lit digits of the alarm clock on the bedside table and relief poured through her when she saw there was still time to go back to her flat and change before getting into work for the Breakfast Show.

Flopping back onto the pillows she ran a hand over her tired eyes.

What had she been thinking?

She never should have done this—allowed her yearning for him to cloud her judgement—surely it could only lead to pain and heartache. He wanted different things to her—had a different life somewhere else. One that he clearly still hadn't come to terms with changing on him. She was just a distraction.

But she wanted to be more. So much more.

And she couldn't give him up now.

Sitting up in bed and flicking on the side light, she saw that Tristan had left the door to the en-suite bathroom open and she could make out the blurred shape of him through the semi-opaque glass of the shower screen.

Her skin immediately heated as she remembered how his body had been wrapped around her the night before, driving her wild.

Too wild.

She was going to have to find a way to keep her sexual and emotional needs separate if she was going to survive this.

The water shut off and she pulled the sheet tighter around her as he came back into the bedroom, a towel slung low on his lean hips and his amazingly honed body sleek with moisture.

'Morning,' he said, giving her one of those killer smiles that made her heart beat faster and heat rush straight between her legs.

She should leave before she lost her cool.

'I really should get going or we'll both be late for work and that would really set tongues wagging,' she said, focussing on getting out of bed with the sheet still wrapped around her so as not to tempt him with her nakedness.

Tristan walked round to her side and pulled the sheet away from her, then gently, but firmly pushed her back onto the bed.

Leaning his strong body forwards he pinned her down onto the mattress.

'No you don't, I'm not ready to let you go yet.' He smiled into her eyes.

'But we'll be late,' she squeaked, just before he brought his mouth down hard onto hers, sending her senses into overload.

'Nah, we've got plenty of time yet,' he mumbled against her lips, sliding his hand down her body to find the needy heat waiting between her thighs. 'Anyway, I'm in with the boss. I'll make sure you don't get fired for being a couple of minutes late.'

Before she could open her mouth to protest about the dubious morals of that sentence, he kissed her again and all rational thought flew right out of her head.

She was very nearly late for work, but managed to squeak in with a couple of minutes to spare.

Luckily, her Broadcast Assistant, Claire, had got the studio ready and had a cup of tea waiting for her. Claire didn't say anything as she handed it over, but Lula could tell from her smile that she suspected something *interesting* had happened last night for her to turn up looking so flushed and flustered.

She somehow got through the show without sounding too flaky, even though every time her thoughts skittered back to Tristan—which was about once every twenty seconds—her body felt like it had burst into flames.

He was waiting outside the studio for her when she came out, leaning against the wall with one leg crossed over the other as if he didn't have a care in the world.

'Lula, can I have a word in my office please?' he said, his expression businesslike and controlled, but she caught the gleam of mischief in his eyes which made her insides tingle with excitement.

Once inside his office, he locked the door and pushed her against it, kissing her passionately, as if they hadn't been allowed to touch each other for weeks rather than a couple of hours.

His enthusiastic attention made her weak at the knees. She'd never felt *desired* like this before and it overrode any hesitancy she had about messing around with him at work.

He was driving her crazy and there was absolutely nothing she could do about it.

Tristan couldn't seem to get enough of her.

Even though he knew she was reluctant to get up to anything in the workplace he couldn't stop himself pushing for it anyway. He enjoyed the excitement of dragging her off into a quiet room and driving her wild with lust until she dropped her weak defences against him.

They made it a whole week, snatching moments at work and seeing each other every evening, either at his place or hers, until it all came crashing down around them.

And it was all his fault.

They'd interviewed another candidate, for what he now thought of as *his* job, the following Monday afternoon.

He hadn't warmed to this woman either, his gut telling him she wasn't quite right for pushing the station forwards and he assumed Lula felt the same way until the excited look on her face registered in his brain.

'She's perfect!' Lula said once the candidate had gone, her eyes shining with glee.

'Seriously?' He frowned, niggled that she would think this woman could do a better job than him.

Not that it *was* his job, he reminded himself. A dull ache throbbed in his chest as he thought about leaving the station in someone else's hands and going back to his business in Scotland. The idea held absolutely no appeal any more. He felt needed here and he'd finally begun to win the staff's respect, which meant a lot to him.

'Look, it's my duty to make sure only the very best

person takes over from me. The place is in enough of a mess after Jez's mishandling of it, it doesn't need someone inexperienced setting it back even further.'

Her look of surprise quickly turned into a frown of annoyance. 'What, like you, you mean?'

'Okay—' he held up a placating hand '—fair enough, I don't have experience in the radio industry, but I know how to run a business and I'm not convinced that this woman does yet. She's only run one small station before and I don't think we can afford to take a leap of faith on her.'

'One small, very successful station that's now winning awards.'

Her face had shut down of emotion and he felt her resistance, like he'd walked into a wall of ice. It only made him want to melt her more.

Getting up from his chair he moved to where she was sitting and knelt down between her legs, pushing them apart to make room for his body and running his hands up the insides of her thighs.

'Are you challenging the boss, Lula?' he growled in his most down and dirty tone, hoping to raise a smile from her. Things had got all too serious here suddenly and he wanted to bring back the levity they'd enjoyed between them for the last week. Even though he'd been aware occasionally that she was struggling with their affair, he'd brushed his concerns to one side, congratulating himself on the fact she couldn't bring herself to stop it.

Just as he couldn't. Despite the voice in his head warning him she needed more from this fling than he was able to give her, he couldn't stop it now. She was like a drug. A very sexy, life-altering drug.

The look in her eyes flickered between annoyance

and lust and he took this as a cue and leant forwards, pressing his lips against hers and lifting one hand to cup the back of her head and stop her from pulling away, until he felt her give in to him.

He didn't register that someone had come into the office until he heard a high, female voice behind him.

'Oh, I'm so sorry, I didn't realise you were *busy* in here.'

Breaking away from Lula, he looked round to see Darla looking at them with an expression of pure disgust on her face.

Something hard and heavy fell in his chest.

He backed away from Lula quickly, standing up and running a hand through his hair, as if neatening himself up would take away the image Darla had just seen.

Idiot.

'What can I do for you, Darla?' he said, trying to force authority into his voice, but she clearly wasn't impressed.

'There's a salary issue I need to discuss with you,' she said coldly, her harsh gaze flicking between him and Lula.

'Okay.' He nodded stiffly. 'I'm just discussing something with Lula, I'll come and find you when we're finished here.'

Darla snorted and inclined her head a fraction, her eyebrows shooting up, suggesting she knew exactly what they were going to *finish*. 'Fine.' She turned on her heel and stomped out, banging the door closed behind her.

He turned to find Lula had stood up and was clutching her hands together in front of her, her eyes wild.

'Dammit!' she said quietly, not meeting his eye.

'Lula, I'm so sorry. I shouldn't have done that without checking the door was locked first.'

She shook her head. 'We shouldn't have done it at all. So unprofessional.' Her voice was low with self-disgust.

'It was my fault. I'll smooth things over with Darla. Offer her a wage hike or something.'

Lula gave him an incredulous look. 'You think you can buy your way out of this?'

He tensed in annoyance. 'I don't know, maybe?'

She looked so offended he had to fold his arms against the power of her glare.

'I'm such an idiot. This is never going to work between us. Not if you think money is going to solve everything and *certainly* not if you think it's okay to try and get your own way by seducing me into retracting my professional opinion.'

He took a deep, sudden breath in response, the force of it burning his throat. 'That's not what I was trying to do.'

'Isn't it? Really? You weren't trying to shut me up by kissing me?'

He didn't reply.

Because she was right.

She gave him one last, hard look before straightening her clothes and leaving the room.

He stared after her, feeling like the lowest of all lowlifes.

She was absolutely correct of course, he did have a problem with relinquishing his control over things—over everything. He was so used to stepping in and taking over, like he had with his family's business—using money or charm to get his way—that he'd acted that way towards Lula without thinking.

And he'd screwed everything up.

* * *

What the hell was she thinking?

She could never work for Tristan when he had the power to overrule anything she said or did just by touching her. To silence her. She'd been a fool to think otherwise.

And now Darla was bound to tell everyone at the station what she'd seen and once again she'd be the centre of whispered gossip and speculation. She shuddered at the thought.

She appeared to have got herself caught in a vicious circle.

That night, she ignored Tristan's calls and pretended to be out when he knocked on her door for ten minutes straight, her chest tight with sorrow. It was never going to work between them. He seemed reluctant to give up his job managing the station, which he appeared to value more than his relationship with her, and she couldn't keep working for him when that was the case.

Not that she hadn't known from the beginning that this was doomed to fail.

After spending her teenage years being passed from parent to parent like a troublesome pet that nobody wanted any more she needed to feel part of something solid. To be with someone who was willing to make gestures that made her feel safe and wanted and cared for. Not someone who was happy to ride roughshod over her opinions and integrity to get his own way.

And he'd made it perfectly clear he wasn't the type to get married. Considering the way her heart had plummeted when she'd heard him say that, she knew a relationship with him would never survive.

She couldn't be with someone who wasn't prepared to put themselves on the line for her. It mattered too much. Even if Emily thought it was a mad whim and told her repeatedly she was living in the dark ages to expect a piece of paper to keep a relationship together. Lula still wanted it. She wanted the promise of it. The romance.

To be loved so much by the person that she was in love with, he was prepared to take the leap of faith with her.

The show the next day was a tough one to get through. It felt as though her head was full of rocks and her mojo was hiding somewhere in the depths of her soul.

'Hey, what's with all the dirgey music?' Claire asked when she brought Lula her fourth cup of coffee into the studio while a track was playing.

'It's a minor key kind of day, Claire. I'm expressing my melancholy.'

Claire paused and gave her a discerning look. 'Does this have something to do with Tristan, by any chance?'

Lula glanced round sharply, blood rushing to her face. 'What do you mean?'

'Well, Darla's been shooting her mouth off about finding you and Tristan—' She gave an uncomfortable cough. 'Being friendly with each other in his office.'

Lula's brow pinched uncomfortably under her frown. 'You know about that?'

Apparently Tristan hadn't been able to buy Darla off.

'Yeah.' She held up a hand. 'Not that I blame you, he's a total honey.'

Lula sighed and dropped her head into her hands. 'I guess everyone thinks I'm a terrible tart who gets what she wants by sleeping with her bosses?' She screwed up her face as she looked back at Claire, not really wanting to hear the answer, but unable to stop herself from asking the question.

Claire wrinkled her nose in surprise. 'What! Don't be ridiculous. Everyone here loves you, they want to see you happy and if that means having a hot fling with Tristan then fine, do it. We know you'd never screw us over, Lula, you're too much of a professional for that.'

'Really?'

'Yes. Of course.'

'I don't know if I can do it any more though, Claire. I don't feel like I have any control or power in this relationship.'

Claire shrugged. 'Well, maybe when he's found someone to take over the running of the station that won't be a problem any more?'

'Maybe. But there's also the small matter of an ex-girlfriend that I don't think he's over yet.'

'Really? You'd never have guessed. He doesn't take his eyes off you for one second when you're in the same room together. If you ask me, he's one smitten kitten.'

Lula stared at her in surprise. 'You think so?'

'Absolutely. I say, go for it.' She gave Lula a wink. 'I would.' Flashing her one last smile, she waltzed out of the studio, letting the heavy soundproof door close with a *swish* behind her.

Lula stared into space, thinking about what she'd just heard. Could that be right?

She had no idea. She appeared to have lost all sense of reality.

Tristan was in his office trying to take his mind off Lula's wall of silence when Flora the receptionist poked her head round his office door.

'Tristan, there's a phone call for you on line one. He said he's your father.'

He stared at her for a moment before coming to his senses. His father? He must have cut his isolated honeymoon short and picked up the message he'd left about firing Jez.

Picking up the handset, he cleared his throat then pressed the button to connect him to line one. 'Dad?'

'Tristan. I'm surprised to find you still there. I thought you'd be back in Edinburgh by now.'

'No, no, still here, fire fighting for your business.' He couldn't keep the scathing tone out of his voice.

His father let out a long, disgruntled sigh. 'Why the hell did you fire Jez? I wanted the DJ to be moved on, not him.'

Tristan's skin prickled with annoyance. 'Well, I've saved you a lot of money and pain by getting rid of him. I'm sorry to land it on you like this, but Jez has been embezzling from the radio station for quite some time.'

There was a tense silence in which Tristan tapped a pen against the desk, waiting for his father to explode with indignation.

'Yeah, I know about that.'

Tristan stared at the pen in his hand, stunned, thinking he must have misheard. 'You knew?'

'Yes.' His father let out another long sigh. 'I set him up there as a favour to his father. When your mother died I did rather a bad job of keeping the business going and Jack, his father, bailed me out. I owe him. He asked me to offer Jez this job to get the lazy sod out of his world of philandering and debauchery and give him a purpose—he wouldn't have taken any help from his own father. I've known for some time that he's been stealing from the company, but it was my way of paying Jack back so I let it slide.'

'Right.' Tristan had no idea how to respond to this. 'So, what happens to the station now?'

'I don't suppose Jez will want to return after being so roundly outed by you so I'll shut it down.' From the sound of his voice he was clearly fed up with the whole mess.

Tristan's heart thumped hard against his chest as he realised what this meant for the staff that he'd taken under his wing for the last month.

And for Lula and her dream show.

'Can't you sell it?' He knew, even as he asked this, that it wasn't an option. There was no value in the station; it was saddled with too much debt.

His father seemed to be thinking along the same lines. 'No point. I'm still stuck in Bangkok but I'll be back in two days and I'll close it down then. Give everyone a redundancy payoff. You'll be able to get back to Scotland by the weekend.'

'Will you sell it to me?' Tristan asked before his father could ring off.

His father snorted in surprise. 'You really want to take it on?'

'Yes.'

There was a silence. 'Okay. Sure. If you want.'

'I do.'

'Okay then. Consider it yours. We'll work out the details when I'm back.'

'Thank you.'

His father laughed quietly. 'I don't know what you're thanking me for, but okay.'

'How was your honeymoon?' Tristan said, realising in his anxiety about the station that he hadn't even asked about it.

'Oh fine. A bit boring being out in the middle of nowhere, but we made our own fun.'

Tristan tried to wipe the icky mental images his father had just implanted from his mind.

'Great, well love to—?'

'Susie.'

'Susie, yeah. Have a good trip back.'

'Will do.'

His father rang off and Tristan put the phone down and stared at the wall.

What had he done? Something crazy and very unbusinesslike. But it felt good. It felt like the right thing to do.

Getting up, he strolled to the door, feeling invigorated with a new sense of purpose.

He needed to find Lula and tell her what was happening.

He found her in one of the small offices, taking some quiet time after her show and she looked at him with a wary expression on her face as he entered the room. His heart turned over as he wondered what sort of reaction he was going to get when he told her the news.

He hoped a positive one, but it was hard to tell with Lula. She always managed to surprise him.

That was one of the things he liked most about her.

Lula's heart-rate picked up as Tristan strolled into the room. She sat up straight, attempting to compose herself for whatever was about to play out.

After giving him the cold shoulder since the *incident* in his office the day before, she wasn't sure what state their relationship was in any more. Or whether she'd still have a job by the end of the day. After all, the last time she'd stood up to her boss, she'd found herself unemployed.

The thought of him firing her now, after all they'd been though, made her feel sick. But more than that, the idea that he might give up on what they had and waltz back off to Scotland drained all the spirit out of her.

She'd had to draw the line with him though, otherwise she was just some sap he'd used and left behind and she wasn't prepared to be that girl. Not any more.

He perched on the edge of the sofa she'd been lying on and blew out a low breath before speaking. 'I just spoke to my father. He wants to shut the station down now that Jez has gone.'

Her heart nearly stopped at the unexpectedly awful news and she sat up so straight her neck clicked. 'What! Why?'

'It's a long story which involves my father being useless and naïve, but before you panic,' he held up a palm, 'there's a solution.'

Her heart rate slowed a little. 'He's going to put it on the market? Or whatever you do with a company.'

He shook his head and frowned, fixing her with a steady stare. 'No one's going to want to buy it in its current state, the debts are too large and it doesn't make enough profit for it to be a going concern.'

He paused and a cold chill ran down her spine.

'So what does that mean?'

His face was devoid of any expression. This was pure business. 'The best thing for the station is for me to buy it and keep it until it breaks even, then look at finding another investor or buyer for it.'

'Will you hand over the day to day managing to

someone else?' she asked hopefully. Perhaps she could deal with that, if he was going to be more hands-off.

But she could tell from the look on his face that he didn't want to do that. He loved running the station. She'd seen first-hand how he thrived on the buzz of the place and how much better it was running now he was in charge.

It was good for him and he was good for it.

'It's probably best if I keep managing it too.'

She took a deep breath. 'How long will it take for it to break even?'

'I don't know. I'll have to look at streamlining the staff and there may need to be lay-offs, but based on the initial sums I've done, maybe years.'

'Years.' She put a hand up to her face and rubbed her temple as another horrible thought struck her. 'I'm the most expensive person here,' she muttered, recalling how her salary had skyrocketed when she took on the Breakfast Show. *Flash* could probably retain the rest of the staff if she was off the payroll.

She stood up, and turned for the door, not wanting him to see her face. 'Actually, this has all come at an opportune time. I've been offered a job in Australia, a really good job, and I've decided to take it.' She couldn't look at him in case he saw the pain in her eyes. 'You'll be able to keep everyone else on here if you're not having to pay me.'

'What the hell? Where did this come from?' He advanced on her and she backed against the wall, her blood pounding in her head, making her feel light-headed.

She held up a hand. 'Truth is, I can't do this any more—pretend I don't want things to work out with you—because I do, and it's going to drive me crazy to never be able to have what I want.'

'What *do* you want, Lula?' His voice was deep and low and fierce.

She raised her gaze to look him dead in the eye. 'The hope that you might want to get married to me one day,' she blurted. 'To have an equal partnership and a strong unit for my children that I never felt I had. For you to put a relationship with me before everything else. Even your commercial empire.'

He looked as though she'd slapped him round the face. 'This is about me not wanting to get *married*.'

'Ultimately, yes.'

Rubbing a hand over his face, he huffed out a dry laugh. 'I think my head might be about to explode.'

Tears welled in her eyes at the flippant way he was dealing with something that meant so much to her.

'If you couldn't bring yourself to marry the woman who was "perfect for you" then Lord knows I don't stand a chance,' she whispered, her chin trembling as she tried to hold it together.

He frowned. 'Hang on, are you talking about Marcy?'

'I can't be your rebound woman, Tristan. I care about you too much for that.'

He didn't respond, just stared at her open-mouthed for a few beats longer.

She nodded once, knowing he couldn't—or wouldn't—give her the reassurance she longed to hear, before pushing past him and walking away.

CHAPTER TEN

TRISTAN STARED OUT of the window as his plane flew over the rolling hills of Northern England on its way to Edinburgh, and reflected on the insight that had struck him hard in the middle of the night: that what he needed was to get some sort of closure there so he could move forwards again.

If he wasn't going to spend the rest of his life messed up and alone he needed to get past the anger and frustration that had been dogging him for months—no, truthfully, *years*—now.

Standing on the doorstep to his brother's and Marcy's house a couple of hours later was both nerve-racking and bolstering. Before this point, even the thought of seeing either of them had been untenable, so this was definitely a positive step forwards.

The look on Marcy's face when she opened the door to him was a picture. Her mouth dropped open and her eyes nearly popped out of her head. 'Tristan!'

He waited for the thud of bitter resentment to hit him, but it didn't come. Strangely, looking at her now, she seemed kind of ordinary, like the sparkle she used to project had gone. 'Hi, Marcy, can I come in?'

She glanced behind her into the house as if checking for backup. 'Jon isn't here. He'll be back in a few minutes though.'

'That's okay, I'll wait. I need to talk to you both.'

After hesitating for a couple of seconds she nodded and opened the door wider so he could walk inside.

She led him into the living room and stood there awkwardly while he looked around at the ultra-modern interior. 'Nice place.'

'Thanks.'

She clapped her hands together awkwardly and stared out of the window.

'Why didn't you ever tell me you were unhappy, Marcy?' he said.

She gave him such a look of disbelief he wondered for a second whether he'd accidentally sworn at her or something. 'I tried, Tristan, but you were always too busy to take my concerns seriously.'

He stared at her in confusion. 'There were plenty of opportunities to talk to me and you know it.'

'Were there?' She sighed and glared down at the ground. 'Look, I'm sorry things happened the way they did. I didn't handle the situation well, I know that.'

His blood pressure rose at her blatant understatement. Clearly he still felt some resentment towards them then, although nothing like the anger he'd been experiencing for the last few months. His shoulders slumped as he took in her drawn expression. 'Yeah, well. What's done is done. I was the idiot that didn't notice what was happening right under my nose.'

She took a step forwards with her hands outstretched. 'I didn't mean to hurt you, Tristan. I seriously thought you wouldn't care about us splitting up.'

He pinched his brows together so hard it hurt. 'You thought I wouldn't *care*?'

She threw her hands up. 'You shut down on me, Tristan, kept me at arm's length. You made me believe there wasn't a future for us when you refused to even discuss getting married.'

'But you knew how I felt about that when we first got together. I was always straight with you, Marcy.'

'I know and I thought it would be enough for me, but then I realised it wasn't and we kept drifting further and further apart as I got angrier about it.' She looked at him fiercely now. 'Jon made me feel wanted.'

Her obvious contempt for Tristan's lack of skill in that department stung, leaving an uncomfortable pressure in his chest. 'Yeah, he was always good at giving people what they want.'

Marcy frowned. 'Look, he feels awful about all this too.'

Tristan closed his eyes and let out a long breath. Now he was here with Marcy he was surprised by how little he felt for her, especially when he compared it to how he felt about Lula. While he'd always found Marcy attractive and smart and good company she hadn't excited him the way Lula excited him.

After having been so caught up in the humiliation of being rejected and lied to, he'd lost sight of the fact he hadn't actually missed Marcy at all and by coming here he was finally coming to terms with that part of his life being over now. He was moving on from anger to acceptance.

Lula's face flashed into his mind as he thought about what Marcy had said about him refusing to even talk about getting married. Her expression had been pretty similar when he'd told her the same thing.

The pressure in his chest increased as he remembered how she'd walked out on him.

She thought he was a lost cause too.

No wonder she was keeping him at arm's length.

He focussed back on Marcy, willing the tightness in his chest to recede. 'Look, Jon's not exactly my favourite person right now, but I'm not going to snub him for ever. We're family and we need to stick together.'

He ran a hand over his hair. 'I've thought of a way he can make things right between us and hopefully set himself up well for the future too.'

'Really? You're finally going to give him the opportunity to help you run the family business? Because he's always felt like a spare part there.'

Tristan sighed. It was a good point, he'd never let Jon take the reins at any point—he'd been too stubborn to delegate any of the responsibility, and that probably went some way to explaining why his brother hadn't bothered coming in to work much. He hadn't allowed him to have any of the control.

'Look, I know I've not handled things well either. I should have talked to both of you more and asked for help instead of pretending everything was okay. And I'm sorry for leaving it so long before re-establishing contact, but I needed a bit of time to hate the both of you before I got on with my life.'

Marcy nodded and gave him a watery smile. 'I understand.'

'Yeah,' Tristan said, his mind suddenly clearer than it had been in years. 'I think I do too.'

He'd been an idiot, assuming everything would work out fine with Lula too if he just ignored the fact she was dead set on getting married and having her happy ever after. Something he hadn't thought he was capable of giving her when they first met.

But she'd made the effort to stand up to him, unlike

Marcy who had just given up on their relationship without letting him know why.

Lula wasn't a coward. She was the bravest woman he'd ever met. He knew he could be formidable when he put his mind to it but she hadn't put up with his crap.

He'd spent so much of his life hardening himself against caring too deeply about other people, in case they left him too, that he'd become a hollow shell of his former self.

Money had become his first and only love and look how that had left him—lonely and bitter.

Now he thought about it, the thing he'd found hardest about Marcy leaving him had been how unprepared he'd been when she'd wrenched away his control. He'd spent his entire life keeping things on track, determined not to live his life in the kamikaze fashion his father did, but he realised he'd missed out on so much by not taking risks. Marcy had left him and he'd survived and now he was on the cusp of losing Lula because of his inability to let go of the stranglehold he had on his life.

He wasn't prepared to let that happen.

He was sure about Lula.

He loved her.

Nothing was guaranteed in this life—the perfect relationship didn't exist—but he wanted to believe he was strong enough in character to stick by his choices and work through any hiccoughs. His father might not be able to do it, but that didn't mean he couldn't.

'Uurgh! Em, what have I done? I'm made a royal mess of everything!' Lula moaned into her sofa cushion, as Emily rubbed soothing circles on her back.

They'd spent the morning together and Lula had become increasingly depressed about the hot mess her life had become.

'Whatever possessed me to talk to a man I've barely even been dating for a few weeks about *getting married*. No wonder he's kept a low profile since then, I probably scared the bejeezus out of him.'

'Clearly it needed to be said though, Lu. You couldn't have gone on hoping things would just work out all fine and dandy without letting him know what you needed out of a relationship. Although, point taken about coming off as a little bit needy.'

'A little bit!' Lula grimaced. 'No wonder I don't seem to be able to hold onto a man.'

Emily batted a hand at her. 'Aah, you just have very high expectations.'

Lula buried her head in the sofa again. 'But I really liked him, Em.' She looked up at her friend, unable to stop the tears from welling in her eyes. '*Really* liked him.' She picked a bit of lint of the cushion. 'In fact, I think I'm in love with him.'

Emily gave her a weak smile and gently rubbed her arm in sympathy. 'Yeah, I know, babe, that's pretty obvious.'

The loud rasp of the buzzer made them both jump.

'You expecting someone?' Emily asked, already levering herself off the sofa.

'No.'

'I'll get rid of them,' Emily said, striding purposefully towards the door. Sometimes Lula was extraordinarily glad of her friend's no-nonsense approach to life. It made her feel safe and protected; something she'd never had a sense of in her youth.

She sank back into the cushions, listening to the low rumble of voices at the door, wondering who it could be.

She didn't have to wonder for long as Emily strode back in with tense shoulders and a *guess who?* expression on her face with Tristan following closely behind her.

All Lula could think in those moments was *he's here* and her heart soared with hope.

'Sorry, Lu, I told him you didn't want to see him, but he wouldn't take no for an answer.' She turned back to scowl at Tristan, but he totally ignored her.

'Lula, I need to speak to you,' Tristan said, taking a step past Emily, towards where she sat on the sofa, his dominating presence seeming to take over the whole room.

'I hope you're here to persuade her to stay, because you'd be an idiot to let someone as amazing as Lula walk away,' Emily said behind him, folding her arms and glaring at the back of Tristan's head.

He turned to meet Emily's gaze and held it, the air crackling with angry tension between them.

It was like watching two stags vying for supremacy.

Lula put up a calming hand to her friend. 'Thanks, Em, but I can handle this on my own.'

Emily narrowed her eyes at Tristan. 'Okay, but you'd better not let her just skip off to Oz or you'll have me to answer to,' she said, finally breaking eye contact with him and walking over to Lula to give her a hug.

'I'm only a phone call away if you need me,' she murmured into her ear, before pulling away and shooting Tristan one last warning frown.

Tristan dipped his head and raised a brow. 'Nice seeing you again,' he said, his voice laden with sarcasm, as Emily spun on her heel and walked out of the room, slamming the front door behind her.

He turned his dark gaze on Lula and she had to fight

back her surge of nerves so as not to turn into a complete gibbering wreck.

'God help any man trying to get close to her, that's all I can say,' he muttered, shaking his head in apparent amusement.

Lula twisted her fingers together. 'Em's had a pretty tough life so she's a bit defensive, but she's a really caring, lovely person when you get to know her.'

He flashed a smile. 'I guess she must be okay if you like her.'

'*Are* you here to persuade me not to leave?' she managed to say past the lump in her throat. 'Because I don't see any presents or cryptic notes.'

He huffed out a laugh. 'It's just me this time. I was hoping that would be enough.'

She broke eye contact and stared at her lap. 'I can't work for you any more, Tristan.'

He paced across the room, shrugging off his coat and hanging it on the peg by her door before returning to her sofa and sitting down next to her.

So he wasn't accepting her resignation then.

Leaning his elbow against the back of the sofa, he propped his head against his hand and studied her for a moment.

Her blood pounded in her throat as she waited for him to say his bit and she picked at a thread on the cushion so she didn't have to look at him.

'I've been thinking about how empty my life would be if you moved to Australia,' he said finally.

Her gaze snapped to his and she pinched her brows together. 'Well, you should be kept pretty busy here in London at the radio station.'

He sighed. 'Lula, I'm not going to move to London if you're not here.'

She could actually hear the blood pulsing through her head. 'Really?'

'No, of course not. It's a Lula-sized hole in my life that I'm concerned about, not a London-sized one.'

She was actually trembling with hope now. 'So, what are you saying?'

'*Flash* can't afford to lose you, Lula. Our audiences love you—the ratings for your show prove that—and we need you to stay to bring in the advertisers. I'll have a monetary stake in the station but be hands-off in the running of it. I'll get someone in to manage it so you won't have to deal with me being your boss any more.'

He was giving up managing the station? 'But you love working at *Flash*.'

The fierce expression in his eyes made her heart flip. 'Actually, it's more that I've enjoyed doing something that *isn't* working for the family business. Thing is, I've been so focused on working there over the years I've let it take priority over everything else in my life.'

He leant his back against the sofa and stared up at the ceiling. 'It was originally my mum's family's business—she met my dad when he started working for them—but when she died my dad lost interest in running it because of his obsession with finding a replacement for her and it got into financial trouble. Apparently Jez's father helped him out of a hole by loaning him money, which is why he was so keen to keep Jez on at *Flash*—as a way to pay his friend back for the gesture.'

'So that's how he managed to get away with so much.'

Tristan raised an eyebrow. 'Yeah. Anyway, I took up the reins at the family business once I'd graduated from Uni because my dad had let it get into trouble again and I couldn't bear to see it fail. My mum would have been devastated. Her father worked so hard to build it up from the ground and I've been trying to keep it alive in memory of her. I felt like it was the only thing I had left of her.'

She had to fight against the tears she wanted to spill for him. 'I bet she would have been proud of you.'

The sadness in his smile nearly broke her heart.

There was an uncomfortable pause where he seemed to be thinking about what she'd said.

He snapped the growing tension by swiping a hand in the air, as if trying to swat away the melancholy. 'Anyway, I put myself under a lot of pressure to keep the business thriving and everything else in my life took a back seat. Like my relationship with Marcy. I never wanted to commit to her because that would have meant putting something other than the business first. That's when my brother stepped in and offered her what she wanted.' He frowned hard.

'Do you think you'll ever make up with him?' she asked gently.

He turned to look at her, dropping the frown. 'Actually, I already have. He's going to take over managing the family business from now on.' His smile was rueful this time. 'It'll do him good to take responsibility for something instead of letting everyone else carry him.'

Lula took a breath, steeling herself to ask the question that played heavily on her mind. 'Are you still in love with Marcy?'

Tristan seemed to consider her question for a few moments, in which her heart hammered so hard against her chest she felt sure he'd be able to hear it.

'I thought it was a good relationship at the time because we never seemed to argue, but the truth was, we weren't around each other enough to have anything real to argue about. And if we did, I bought her things I thought she wanted—material possessions—to smooth things over. I gave her everything she ever asked for. Except my undivided attention and love.'

He huffed out a laugh. 'She said I didn't see her as a person, only a commodity. I didn't understand what she meant until I met you. Until you forced me to think about you as an individual, instead of something to be bought off and placated. You made getting to know someone real for me, by making me care about you.'

The irrefutable look of hope on Lula's face made him want to pull her against him and never let her go, but he needed to say more—to explain himself— before he got distracted by the urge to haul her off to bed and *show* her how much he cared.

He laid his hand on her leg, asking for a chance to say what he needed to without interruption and she nodded, encouraging him on.

His heart beat like a jackhammer against his chest as he gathered his courage.

'When my dad got married again and I let myself love my new stepmother I felt as though I was being disloyal to my mum.'

He glanced at her and she nodded, the empathy in her eyes telling him she understood.

'Then my stepmother left and I felt stupid for being so quick to let myself care about her. I missed my mum so much, and I'd wanted someone to fill the gaping hole she'd left, so I threw myself into caring for the first person that came along to bridge it. After it happened *again* I started disengaging my emotions from my stepmothers altogether.'

'I can understand why you'd react like that.'

He squeezed her leg, knowing she really *did* get where he was coming from and loving her for it. 'The worst thing, I realise now, was that I started to do it with my girlfriends too. It was a bad habit that I didn't realise I had until you came along and pointed it out to me. Marcy hadn't been able to penetrate my wall of emotional iron and gave up on me, but you made me think about how things were affecting *you*, first of all by forcing me to work hard to get you to take your job back. Then as soon as I'd begun to think about you as a real person, instead of just a faceless employee, you worked your way under my skin. As I got to know and like you I fell for you more and more and it scared the crap out of me.'

'I can't imagine you being afraid of anything. You're so self-possessed.'

He raised a brow. 'Not so much. Hence all the controlling behaviour recently. I was trying to find a way to get on top of this *fear* you'd triggered.'

Her eyes were wide. 'I never meant to make you feel like that. I know I can be a bit challenging.'

'I needed you to challenge me. Thing is, I've always cushioned my life with money, which gave me a sense of protection and safety, but it never made me happy. In fact it only made me more protective and less open to taking risks, especially with my relationships. I've spent most of my life using money to smooth my way through things, but you're the one thing I couldn't buy and that totally messed with my head. In a good way.'

She snorted and looked down at where his hand still lay hot and heavy on her leg. 'I thought I'd scared you off for good by practically demanding we get married.'

'It wasn't the marriage thing that scared me, that was an excuse, it was the sentiment behind it—the act of giving myself completely to someone else that I struggled with. Because when I promise something, I don't go back on my word. It's for ever, and for ever is a long time to be with someone if you're not sure about them, especially if you have children relying on you to get it right. I don't want my kids to go through the hell of losing parent after parent like I did. It's not fair.'

'My thoughts exactly.' She was nodding hard, her eyes lit up with hope.

He knew he had to be with her, even if it meant giving up his tight control on life. In fact, he *wanted* to let go for her. To experience new things that both scared and excited him—as long as she was along for the ride. He wanted to do it all with her.

He'd never been able to picture himself with Marcy long-term, but he realised he couldn't imagine himself *without* Lula now. Just the thought of it made his chest contract painfully.

'To answer your question, I'm not in love with Marcy. But I *am* in love with you.'

Her gaze slid away from his and he could feel her trembling under his touch.

He balked as he realised she wasn't giving him the joyful response he was hoping for.

'Lula? What's wrong?'

Her eyes were full of fear when she looked back at him. 'I'm sacred that you don't really know me, Tristan. You only know the Tallulah I've been showing you and when you get to know the real me you'll be disappointed.'

He frowned hard and moved closer to her, to reassure her that wasn't the case. Couldn't be. 'What you've shown me *is* you, Lula. I know you think you've been pretending to be something you *think* everyone wants, but you couldn't have been that person if it wasn't in you to begin with—the sparky, funny, quirky *you* that you keep hidden until you trust someone.'

He put a hand on her cheek and tipped her face so she had to keep looking him in the eye. 'That's one of the things I love about you—that you have a secret side that you only let certain people see. I think, without you realising, you've already let me be one of those people. When we first met, *Louise* was the mask that let you be yourself. You showed me the truth when you were pretending to be her because you could blame any shortcoming on her. You could hide behind her faults, rather than your own. It's a classic deflection technique. I've seen every side of you, Lula, and I love them all. I'm not going anywhere.'

'Really?' she said, clearly trying not to cry.

'Yes, really.' He smiled and brushed a rogue tear away from under her eye. 'You know, I think I'm finally beginning to understand my father's addiction to falling in love. The first flush is like the most intense happiness drug. But, unlike my father it's not the be-all and end-all for me. I want to grow to love you in all the ways possible, even when we're angry with each other. I can't imagine ever wanting to be without you.'

She took a deep shaky breath. 'Me neither because I love you too.' She was telling the truth, he could see the certainty in her eyes.

The great weight of fear lifted as he heard her say those words.

'Then don't go to Australia. Stay here and marry me. *Flash* will be *our* station. I'll make you a shareholder. We'll hire the candidate you liked to manage it day to day but we'll both have an equal say in how it's run.'

She stared at him in shock. 'You're asking me to marry you?'

'Yes.'

She frowned. 'But we've only known each other for a month.'

'Doesn't matter. It's what I want. You're what I want.'

'I can't believe you'd do that for me.' Her voice wobbled with emotion.

'For us.'

She shook her head and moved away from where his hand rested on her cheek, drawing herself up straight. 'We don't have to get married. Just the fact you've asked me to, because you think it would make me happy is enough. I know being married doesn't necessarily mean we'll be together for ever, but I needed to know you were prepared to make a promise that cost you something to say. I believe that you love me. And I love you. That's enough for me.'

'Well, let's keep it as an open discussion. We don't have to decide anything right now. I just want to be with you, Lula. And I want you to always feel that you can talk to me, even when we're angry with each other.'

He cupped her face again and stroked his thumb across her soft, full lips. 'Please don't think you have to withdraw into your own head again, it would kill me to think I'd made you do that.'

This time she gave him a genuine smile and he knew it was going to be okay. They'd make it work, because it was what they both wanted.

'Okay. I promise,' she said, leaning forward to kiss him gently. 'No more silence.'

EPILOGUE

One year later

LULA HAD JUST wrapped up her breakfast show and handed over the reins to the next presenter when her Broadcast Assistant buzzed through to let her know that Tristan was on the phone for her.

She picked up the line in the studio, already smiling at the thought of hearing his voice. He'd nearly made her late again that morning by dragging her back into bed after her shower and she was still buzzing, and a little sore—in the best way possible—from his intensive attention.

'Hello, beautiful, great show,' he said, the sound of his voice sending waves of lustful need straight to those still aching parts of her.

'Thank you. How come you were listening? I thought you had a meeting with your new programmer this morning?'

Tristan's new educational open source software enterprise had gone from strength to strength since he'd set it up a year ago and it was unusual for him to take a working morning off.

'Grab your stuff and come and meet me outside. Don't worry, I've cleared it with Caitlin, she knows I've got plans for you today.'

A zing of excitement travelled up her spine. 'What plans?'

'You'll see. Just get your sexy arse out here asap.'

When she emerged into the cool spring air she found him leaning against their car with his arms folded across his broad chest and a wide smile on his handsome face.

'Where are we going?' she asked, desperate to know what he had in store for her. She loved the surprises he cooked up—he had a real knack for knowing exactly what she'd enjoy.

That was one of the things she loved most about him, that he *got* her.

'We're celebrating your Best New Breakfast Radio Show Presenter nomination by going on a road trip. I've booked a room at the Burgh Island Hotel in Devon for tonight.'

'Ooh, I've always wanted to stay there!' she said, the buzz of excitement making her voice squeaky.

He smiled. 'I know.'

Four hours later they had their trouser legs rolled up to their knees and were wading through the cold, shallow seawater between the mainland and Burgh Island.

'We could have taken the tractor across with the luggage,' Tristan said, smirking as he caught her frowning at the icy cold water.

'No, no, I wanted to walk,' she said, teeth chattering, batting away his amusement. 'It's good for the health to get your feet in the cold sea.' She drew in a deep lungful of the briny air and gave him an imperious look.

He raised an eyebrow and snorted. 'You and your factual gobbledegook.'

Even though the sun was shining, the island wasn't busy with tourists and it was so quiet the only sounds they could hear were the gentle lapping of the sea and the cries of the seagulls overhead.

Once they'd made it onto dry land and checked in at the opulent Art Deco hotel, Tristan led her over to the other side of the island so they could look out at the unbroken expanse of sea.

Lula took a deep breath as she gazed out at the endless blue-grey of the horizon. 'It's like being at the edge of the world,' she said.

She turned to smile at him to find he was giving her such a loving look her heart nearly leapt out of her chest.

Before she could say anything else, he surprised her by dropping to his knee and pulling something that looked like a small, black box out of his pocket.

'What are you doing?' she asked, even though she knew.

She knew.

His gaze held hers steadily as he flipped open the box to reveal a square cut diamond ring. It was the most beautiful thing she'd seen in her life.

Words failed her and she began to shake with excitement as she stared at him.

Luckily, Tristan knew exactly what to say.

'I wanted to do this away from the distractions of the city, where it could just be the two of us. Alone together. I love you, Lula, and I want to spend the rest of my life getting to love you a bit more each day. Will you marry me?'

Tears filled her eyes as she experienced the most exquisite sense of peace and serenity. This is how it was meant to be, being here with him on equal terms, being sure, being happy.

'Yes,' she said. 'I will.'

* * * * *